Perfect Stranger

The Millionaire's Pretty Woman Series, Volume 1

Lexy Timms

Published by Dark Shadow Publishing, 2021.

This is a work of fiction. Similarities to real people, places, or events are entirely coincidental.

PERFECT STRANGER

First edition. July 1, 2021.

Copyright © 2021 Lexy Timms.

Written by Lexy Timms.

Also by Lexy Timms

A Bad Boy Bullied Romance
I Hate You
I Hate You A Little Bit
I Hate You A Little Bit More

A Bump in the Road Series
Expecting Love
Selfless Act
Doctor's Orders

A Burning Love Series
Spark of Passion
Flame of Desire
Blaze of Ecstasy

A Chance at Forever Series
Forever Perfect
Forever Desired

Forever Together

A Dark Mafia Romance Series
Taken By The Mob Boss
Truce With The Mob Boss
Taking Over the Mob Boss
Trouble For The Mob Boss
Tailored By The Mob Boss
Tricking the Mob Boss

A Dating App Series
I've Been Matched
You've Been Matched
We've Been Matched

A "Kind of" Billionaire
Taking a Risk
Safety in Numbers
Pretend You're Mine

A Maybe Series
Maybe I Should
Maybe I Shouldn't
Maybe I Did

Assisting the Boss Series
Billion Reasons
Duke of Delegation
Late Night Meetings
Delegating Love
Suitors and Admirers

BBW Romance Series
Capturing Her Beauty
Pursuing Her Dreams
Tracing Her Curves

Beating the Biker Series
Making Her His
Making the Break
Making of Them

Betrayal at the Bay Series
Devil's Bay
Devil's Deceit
Devil's Duplicity

Billionaire Banker Series
Banking on Him

Price of Passion
Investing in Love
Knowing Your Worth
Treasured Forever
Banking on Christmas
Billionaire Banker Box Set Books #1-3

Billionaire CEO Brothers
Tempting the Player
Late Night Boardroom
Reviewing the Perfomance
Result of Passion
Directing the Next Move
Touching the Assets

Billionaire Hitman Series
The Hit
The Job
The Run

Billionaire Holiday Romance Series
Driving Home for Christmas
The Valentine Getaway
Cruising Love
Billionaire Holiday Romance Box Set

Billionaire in Disguise Series
Facade
Illusion
Charade

Billionaire Secrets Series
The Secret
Freedom
Courage
Trust
Impulse
Billionaire Secrets Box Set Books #1-3

Blind Sight Series
See Me
Fix Me
Eyes On Me

Branded Series
Money or Nothing
What People Say
Give and Take

Building Billions

Building Billions - Part 1
Building Billions - Part 2
Building Billions - Part 3

Butler & Heiress Series
To Serve
For Duty
No Chore
All Wrapped Up

Change of Heart Series
The Heart Needs
The Heart Wants
The Heart Knows

Counting the Billions
Counting the Days
Counting On You
Counting the Kisses

Cry Wolf Reverse Harem Series
Beautiful & Wild
Misunderstood
Never Tamed

Darkest Night Series
Savage
Vicious
Brutal
Sinful
Fierce

Diamond in the Rough Anthology
Billionaire Rock
Billionaire Rock - part 2

Dirty Little Taboo Series
Flirting Touch
Denying Pleasure
Forbidding Desire
Craving Passion

Dominating PA Series
Her Personal Assistant - Part 1
Her Personal Assistant - Part 2
Her Personal Assistant Box Set

Fake Billionaire Series
Faking It

Temporary CEO
Caught in the Act
Never Tell A Lie
Fake Christmas
Fake Billionaire Box Set #1-3

Firehouse Romance Series
Caught in Flames
Burning With Desire
Craving the Heat
Firehouse Romance Complete Collection

Forging Billions Series
Dirty Money
Petty Cash
Payment Required

For His Pleasure
Elizabeth
Georgia
Madison

Fortune Riders MC Series
Billionaire Biker
Billionaire Ransom
Billionaire Misery

Fortune Riders Box Set - Books #1-3

Fragile Series
Fragile Touch
Fragile Kiss
Fragile Love

Great Temptation Series
The Devil's Footsteps
Heaven's Command
Mortals Surrender

Hades' Spawn Motorcycle Club
One You Can't Forget
One That Got Away
One That Came Back
One You Never Leave
One Christmas Night
Hades' Spawn MC Complete Series

Hard Rocked Series
Rhyme
Harmony
Lyrics

Heart of Stone Series
The Protector
The Guardian
The Warrior

Heart of the Battle Series
Celtic Viking
Celtic Rune
Celtic Mann
Heart of the Battle Series Box Set

Heistdom Series
Master Thief
Goldmine
Diamond Heist
Smile For Me
Your Move
Green With Envy
Saving Money

Highlander Wolf Series
Pack Run
Pack Land
Pack Rules

Hollyweird Fae Series
Inception of Gold
Disruption of Magic
Guardians of Twilight

How To Love A Spy
The Secret
The Secret Life
The Secret Wife

Just About Series
About Love
About Truth
About Forever
Just About Box Set Books #1-3

Justice Series
Seeking Justice
Finding Justice
Chasing Justice
Pursuing Justice
Justice - Complete Series

Karma Series

Walk Away
Make Him Pay
Perfect Revenge

Kissed by Billions
Kissed by Passion
Kissed by Desire
Kissed by Love

Leaning Towards Trouble
Trouble
Discord
Tenacity

Love on the Sea Series
Ships Ahoy
Rough Sea
High Tide

Love You Series
Love Life
Need Love
My Love

Managing the Billionaire

Never Enough
Worth the Cost
Secret Admirers
Chasing Affection
Pressing Romance
Timeless Memories
Managing the Billionaire Box Set Books #1-3

Managing the Bosses Series
The Boss
The Boss Too
Who's the Boss Now
Love the Boss
I Do the Boss
Wife to the Boss
Employed by the Boss
Brother to the Boss
Senior Advisor to the Boss
Forever the Boss
Christmas With the Boss
Billionaire in Control
Billionaire Makes Millions
Billionaire at Work
Precious Little Thing
Priceless Love
Valentine Love
The Cost of Freedom
Trick or Treat
The Night Before Christmas
Gift for the Boss - Novella 3.5
Managing the Bosses Box Set #1-3

Managing the Bosses Novellas

Mislead by the Bad Boy Series
Deceived
Provoked
Betrayed

Model Mayhem Series
Shameless
Modesty
Imperfection

Moment in Time
Highlander's Bride
Victorian Bride
Modern Day Bride
A Royal Bride
Forever the Bride

Mountain Millionaire Series
Close to the Ridge
Crossing the Bluff
Climbing the Mount

My Best Friend's Sister

Hometown Calling
A Perfect Moment
Thrown in Together

My Darker Side Series
Darkest Hour
Time to Stop
Against the Light

Neverending Dream Series
Neverending Dream - Part 1
Neverending Dream - Part 2
Neverending Dream - Part 3
Neverending Dream - Part 4
Neverending Dream - Part 5
Neverending Dream Box Set Books #1-3

Outside the Octagon
Submit
Fight
Knockout

Protecting Diana Series
Her Bodyguard
Her Defender
Her Champion

Her Protector
Her Forever
Protecting Diana Box Set Books #1-3

Protecting Layla Series
His Mission
His Objective
His Devotion

Racing Hearts Series
Rush
Pace
Fast

Regency Romance Series
The Duchess Scandal - Part 1
The Duchess Scandal - Part 2

Reverse Harem Series
Primals
Archaic
Unitary

R&S Rich and Single Series
Alex Reid

Parker
Sebastian

Saving Forever
Saving Forever - Part 1
Saving Forever - Part 2
Saving Forever - Part 3
Saving Forever - Part 4
Saving Forever - Part 5
Saving Forever - Part 6
Saving Forever Part 7
Saving Forever - Part 8
Saving Forever Boxset Books #1-3

Secrets & Lies Series
Strange Secrets
Evading Secrets
Inspiring Secrets
Lies and Secrets
Mastering Secrets
Alluring Secrets
Secrets & Lies Box Set Books #1-3

Shifting Desires Series
Jungle Heat
Jungle Fever
Jungle Blaze

Sin Series
Payment for Sin
Atonement Within
Declaration of Love

Southern Romance Series
Little Love Affair
Siege of the Heart
Freedom Forever
Soldier's Fortune

Spanked Series
Passion
Playmate
Pleasure

Spelling Love Series
The Author
The Book Boyfriend
The Words of Love

Strength & Style
Suits You, Sir
Tailor Made

Taboo Wedding Series
He Loves Me Not
With This Ring
Happily Ever After

Tattooist Series
Confession of a Tattooist
Surrender of a Tattooist
Heart of a Tattooist
Hopes & Dreams of a Tattooist

Tennessee Romance
Whisky Lullaby
Whisky Melody
Whisky Harmony

The Bad Boy Alpha Club
Battle Lines - Part 1
Battle Lines

The Brush Of Love Series
Every Night
Every Day
Every Time

Every Way
Every Touch
The Brush of Love Series Box Set Books #1-3

The City of Mayhem Series
True Mayhem
Relentless Chaos

The Debt
The Debt: Part 1 - Damn Horse
The Debt: Complete Collection

The Fire Inside Series
Dare Me
Defy Me
Burn Me

The Gentleman's Club Series
Gambler
Player
Wager

The Golden Mail
Hot Off the Press
Extra! Extra!

Read All About It
Stop the Press
Breaking News
This Just In
The Golden Mail Box Set Books #1-3

The Lucky Billionaire Series
Lucky Break
Streak of Luck
Lucky in Love

The Millionaire's Pretty Woman Series
Perfect Stranger
Captive Devotion
Sweet Temptations

The Sound of Breaking Hearts Series
Disruption
Destroy
Devoted

The University of Gatica Series
The Recruiting Trip
Faster
Higher
Stronger

Dominate
No Rush
University of Gatica - The Complete Series

T.N.T. Series
Troubled Nate Thomas - Part 1
Troubled Nate Thomas - Part 2
Troubled Nate Thomas - Part 3

Toxic Touch Series
Noxious
Lethal
Willful
Tainted
Craved
Toxic Touch Box Set Books #1-3

Undercover Boss Series
Marketing
Finance
Legal

Undercover Series
Perfect For Me
Perfect For You
Perfect For Us

Unknown Identity Series
Unknown
Unpublished
Unexposed
Unsure
Unwritten
Unknown Identity Box Set: Books #1-3

Unlucky Series
Unlucky in Love
UnWanted
UnLoved Forever

War Torn Letters Series
My Sweetheart
My Darling
My Beloved

Wet & Wild Series
Stormy Love
Savage Love
Secure Love

Worth It Series

Worth Billions
Worth Every Cent
Worth More Than Money

You & Me - A Bad Boy Romance
Just Me
Touch Me
Kiss Me

Standalone
Wash
Loving Charity
Summer Lovin'
Love & College
Billionaire Heart
First Love
Frisky and Fun Romance Box Collection
Beating Hades' Bikers
Everyone Loves a Bad Boy

Watch for more at www.lexytimms.com.

Perfect Stranger

The Millionaire's Pretty Woman Series #1

USA TODAY BESTSELLING AUTHOR
LEXY TIMMS

Copyright 2021 By LEXY TIMMS

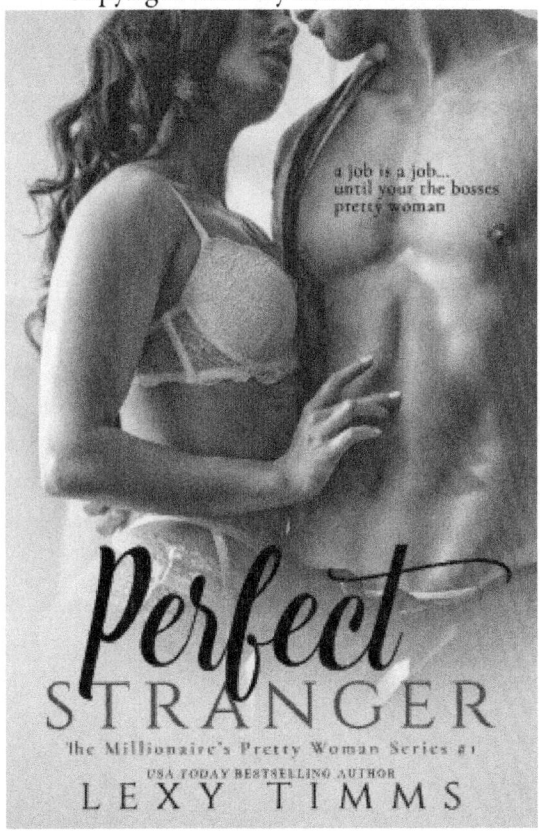

ALL RIGHTS RESERVED. No part of this publication may be reproduced, stored in or introduced into a retrieval system, or transmitted, in any form, or by any means (electronic, mechanical, photocopying, recording, or otherwise) without the prior written permission of both the copyright owner and the above publisher of this book.

This is a work of fiction. Names, characters, places, brands, media, and incidents are either the product of the author's imagination or are used fictitiously. Any resemblance to an actual person, living or dead, events, or locales is entirely coincidental. The author acknowledges the trademarked status and trademark owners of various products referenced in this work of fiction, which have been used without permission. The publication/use of these trademarks is not authorized, associated with, or sponsored by the trademark owners.

· · ⚜ · ·

All rights reserved.
Perfect Stranger
The Millionaire's Pretty Woman Series Book 1
Copyright 2021 by Lexy Timms
Cover by: Book Cover by Design[1]

---

1. http://bookcoverbydesign.co.uk/

The Millionaire's Pretty Woman Series

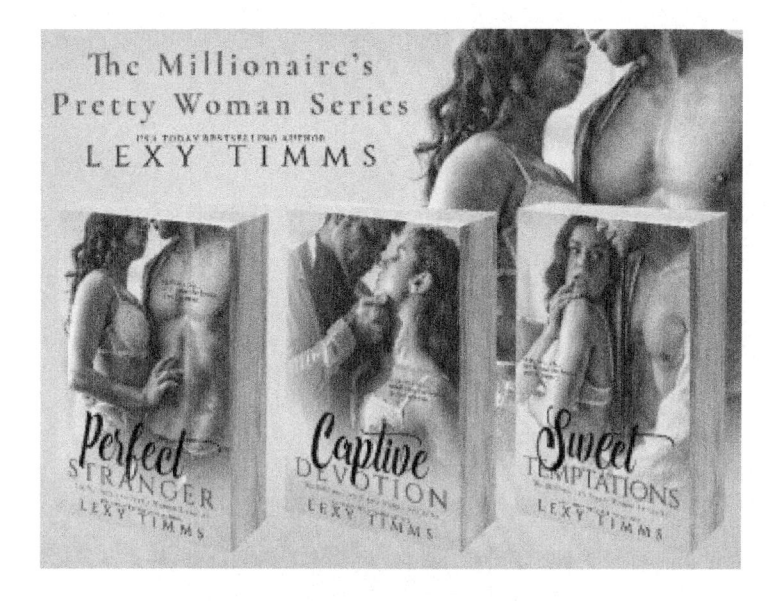

Book 1 – Perfect Stranger
Book 2 – Captive Devotion
Book 3 – Sweet Temptations

Find Lexy Timms:

LEXY TIMMS NEWSLETTER:
http://eepurl.com/9i0vD
Lexy Timms Facebook Page:
https://www.facebook.com/SavingForever
Lexy Timms Website:
http://www.lexytimms.com

Want to read more...
For **FREE?**
Sign up for Lexy Timms' newsletter
And she'll send you updates on new releases, ARC copies of books
and a whole lotta fun!
Sign up for news and updates!
http://eepurl.com/9i0vD

Perfect Stranger Blurb

IN THAT PERFECT STRANGER, I found my fairytale...

Olivia Cadwell, brilliant with numbers but still having trouble figuring out where she fits into the world, is on the run from her hometown, courtesy of her mother's boyfriend—who has decided that Olivia is his next target.

Leo Folley, head of the multi-billion-dollar company his father started, is minding his own business and carrying on as usual... until his publicist gives him a deadline: Find a girlfriend, play nice with the press, and be a better face for the company, or the board is going to make trouble.

When Leo finds Olivia sleeping in her car in the alley outside of his office, he sees the perfect answer to his dilemma: a girl who needs money and a place to stay in exchange for playing his date for the big charity auction. For Olivia, it's the perfect solution: money, a place to stay, and safety from the man she's sure is searching for her. What's not to love?

They both believe they can get through the week without taking anything too seriously.

They're both wrong.
A job is a job, until you're the bosses pretty woman...

CHAPTER 1

LEO

"LET ME GET THIS STRAIGHT. You're saying that I actually have to have a girl on my arm to avoid losing the faith of the board? Losing the company itself?" I asked, stifling the groan I could feel growing in my throat.

"What I'm saying," Meghan, my lead publicist, said coldly, "is that it wouldn't be the worst thing for you to look a little more social. Go out. Act like a real human being rather than just the shadow behind Folley. Show that you have a freaking heart."

She threw a number of newspaper clippings down on the desk in front of me to punctuate her point.

And I released the groan I'd so far been at least trying to hold back.

Then I reached for the clippings, because Meghan was my head publicist, and that meant it was her job to not only tell me the truth about things, but also keep me in line when it came to things like my public image.

Look, I didn't think I should have to worry about that sort of thing. I was the head of a multibillion-dollar company, and we did just fine, thank you very much. The company, a conglomerate of smaller companies that dealt with communications of all shapes and sizes, was like a spinning top, running so smoothly that anyone else should have been jealous.

I didn't see why I should have to do anything other than keep on running it.

"What are these?" I asked, thumbing through the clippings and seeing a whole load of nothing but articles. Articles that featured my name and the name of the company I'd built.

"They're articles," she said sarcastically. "Articles about you." She reached down, grabbed them out of my hands, and spread them across the table. "Articles that talk about how selfish you are, and how rich you are, and how the world itself would be a better place if you would just start sharing that wealth around. Doing good every so often."

I looked up at her, more than a little bit shocked.

"That's awfully rich, considering I give—and the company gives—hundreds of thousands of dollars every year to charity."

She shot a glare my way. "Anonymously. You never put your name on those donations—no matter how many times I've told you that you should—and that right there is the problem, Leo. If you don't put your name on the donations, or at least the company's name, then you're not going to get credit for it."

"I don't need credit," I growled. "That's not what giving to charity is about. It's not like I'm trying to earn tokens for a prize at the end of the game. The minute I start adding my name to it, you and I both know they're going to find something else to complain about. Hell, they'll probably complain that I'm bragging about my own wealth by showing how much I can give away. They'll say I'm just trying to curry favor or that it's a publicity stunt."

She grabbed the newspaper clippings up and shoved them back into the planner she carried everywhere with her.

Seriously, I wouldn't have been surprised if she slept with the fucking thing. I was positive that I'd never seen her without it, and it might as well have been Mary Poppins' handbag. She could fit everything she needed into that thing, regardless of how big or small it was.

"Well, right now it's no kind of publicity at all, and that means it's a waste of time and money," she said sharply.

I snorted. "A waste of money to give money to charity. Got it. I'll note that down in the Official Rulebook According to Meghan."

She made a face at me. "That's not what I mean, and you know it. I'm just saying, Leo. As long as you're making those donations anyhow, you might as well be getting some credit for it. Right now, you're not. And your reputation is taking a hit for it."

I blew out a long breath but kept my mouth shut.

This wasn't the first time I'd heard exactly that, and Meghan wasn't the first person to say it to me.

So I was well aware that this was an... issue.

But even so.

"Okay, so say I agreed to put my name on these donations when I make them," I said, conceding the point. "What the hell does that have to do with having a girl on my arm? Or the board of the company?"

The board... was a problem. When I took the company public, wanting to get fresh blood in the place and fresh eyes on some of the deals we were doing, it had come with a big asterisk. Namely, the board, which now got to vote on most of what I did.

I didn't take them seriously most of the time, because it was still my company. It still sported my name, and I was still the one running it and making everyone else money.

But I preferred to stay on their good side, if I could. Getting along and having a peaceful partnership made my life a whole lot easier.

Also, they could, if they wanted to, vote me out of my position. It was something my own assistant, Janice, and Meghan herself never let me forget.

And even I had to admit that it was a valid threat. Yes, the company was mine. Yes, I'd started it and packed it around on my own back with my own money until it finally started turning a profit. But taking it public had meant signing a deal with the devil.

A deal that had a line it about keeping the damn board happy.

At my question, Meghan reached into her wonder binder and yanked out yet another set of newspaper clippings, tossing them down in front of me with what looked like a bit less anger.

"What did you do, spend your entire night going through newspapers?" I asked, giving her a jaded glance as I took this new set off the desk.

"I've been collecting them for weeks, actually," she replied. "I knew I needed proof if I was going to come in here and tell you that you had to do better."

I narrowed my eyes at her, but then turned them to the clippings without saying anything else.

Shit, there were at least twenty of them. And each of them had not only a photo—of me with some different girl—but also a story about how I was too much of a playboy to take life seriously. How I didn't deserve to run a company so big when I couldn't even settle down with one girl.

How I not only didn't give money to any charities, but also seemed to specialize in being out with a different girl every night.

I closed my eyes, feeling like steam might start pouring out of my ears at any second.

Because a grand total of *none* of those dates had been my idea. I didn't want a girl on my arm—or in my bed, or in my house, rearranging my cupboards or putting lacy curtains up or going through my medicine cabinet. I was quite happy on my own, thank you very much, and I planned to stay that way for as long as I could manage it.

My friends, though, had other ideas. And they'd gone through a phase of setting me up with a different girl every night, partly because they'd thought it was funny, and partly because they were girls they couldn't date on their own.

They'd been living vicariously through me.

"For the record," I muttered, "I wasn't having fun on any of those dates. And none of that was my idea."

"You and I know that," Meghan muttered back. "But no one else seems to. And I can't get a word in edgewise with the press when they decide to talk about your dating habits. You're either out there alone, the loneliest bachelor ever to bachelor, or you've got a different model on your arm every single night." She put her palms down on the desk and leaned toward me, her dark blue eyes incredibly serious. "The end result, Leo, is that we've got a lot of rehab to do on your reputation. The board doesn't like that you're drawing the wrong sort of attention, and Janice and I have both heard murmurings about them taking a vote. It's time to make you friendlier to the public eye."

Well, shit. I hadn't wanted to take her seriously. I'd wanted this to all be some sort of joke.

But I had learned to take her seriously when she looked at me like that. She had never used the board to try to bully me into doing a publicity stunt before.

It made me very, very nervous that she was doing it now.

"So what do we do, oh guru of publicity?" I asked, my own face as serious as hers. "I don't want the board breathing down my neck any more than you do. And I pay you to take care of things like this for me. So what's the plan?"

Finally, she allowed a smile to stretch her lips. "Easy. Start attaching your name to those donations. Get a girl that the press can take more than one picture of. Keep her around for a while—and make sure she's smart enough to handle the paparazzi. Take her to the charity auction next week so there are plenty of pictures of you two. Play the good boy for a month or two." The smile grew and became mischievous. "After that, you can go back to being the curmudgeon who doesn't like going out because he doesn't like to be recognized. I promise."

I lifted my brows. "You're showing me all the pictures the press has taken of me, and yet you're going to shame me for not wanting to go out because of the press and their cameras? Low blow, Meghan."

She leaned in even closer, the grin turning crafty. "Leo, it's my job to make sure your public persona is sparkling and perfect. I use whatever tools I have available to me. Find a girl by the charity auction at the end of the week, or I'll do that for you, too."

She turned on one stiletto heel and was gone before I could point out that I didn't need a matchmaker.

Though to be honest, she probably would have done a better job of finding a girl than I was going to do.

I watched her walk out of my office, my mind still spinning in circles around the idea that I was being required to find a girlfriend—for an evidently unspecified amount of time—and sign my name on the dotted line of my charitable contributions.

Just to please the board.

Look, I'd known when I took them on that it was a double-edged knife. I'd known good and well that there were going to be additional rules and that I'd have to start allowing people other than myself to have a choice in how the company ran.

I just never thought they'd be playing matchmaker for me.

I shook my head, groaned at the thought of actually taking a girl on more than one date—and pretending to like it—and then turned off my computer and got up.

It had been a tough day already, and I had an office at home. An office where neither my publicist or assistant could randomly walk in on me and start issuing demands. I'd get a lot more work done there than I was going to do here.

Because unlike this office, my penthouse was completely devoid of other humans.

And I liked it that way.

CHAPTER 2

OLIVIA

IT HAD TO BE NEARLY ten in the morning when I woke up, and for long, terrifying moments, I couldn't remember where the hell I was... or how the hell I'd gotten there.

Believe me when I say that few things are more terrifying than waking up in a car in an alleyway between towering buildings—which are set on a very noisy street—and having absolutely zero memory of how you'd come to be there.

I went quickly over my body, trying to figure out whether anything was missing—like a kidney, which I'd heard people stole sometimes if they found you under the right circumstances—and quickly came to the conclusion that everything was there and accounted for. All four limbs, attached. No obvious signs of trauma.

No holes in my trunk where my kidneys might once have been.

I could see straight, and my tongue was still in my mouth.

No, I don't know why my tongue would have been missing. But when you also can't remember where you are or why, you tend to check random things, I guess.

Honestly, I'd never been in this situation before, so I didn't know if that was true at all. But it certainly was for me.

I was putting frantic fingers up to my face to see whether that was still attached when my brain finally—finally!—decided to chime in and add to the freaked-out conversation going on in my subconscious.

You, it said coldly, *are a fucking idiot. You know exactly where you are and how you got here, because you drove yourself.*

Drove myself. Right.

Wait, what?

And then, memory. Of everything. I remembered exactly where I was—Minneapolis—and how I'd gotten here—via my car.

Which was one of the only things I'd brought with me when I hightailed it the hell out of Bloomingdale, the town where I'd been living down the street from my mother for the last five years.

Longer than that, actually. I'd been living there my entire life.

Not anymore, though.

I sat my car's seat up and stared blearily through the windshield toward the street at the end of the alley, casting my mind back to the way I'd come screeching into Minneapolis last night, stereo blaring and my eyes still stinging with angry tears.

It had taken me four hours to get here, going eighty the entire way. And four hours hadn't been enough to forget about what had happened in Bloomingdale during the day.

I'd always known that my mother's newest boyfriend, Roger, was a real piece of shit. More than that. He was the kind of guy who raged at her and threatened her constantly... and then turned around and made her think that it was her fault he was doing it. Then he sweet-talked her until she forgot about what an asshole he was.

I had never, however, seen him actually hit her.

Yesterday morning, I'd seen just that. I'd been at their house for breakfast, the way I always was on Sunday mornings, and they'd gotten into yet another fight about one thing or another. It had escalated so quickly that I hadn't been able to get out of the room just to avoid being in the middle of it, the way I always managed to.

So I'd seen him slap her across the face and send her to the ground.

I'd seen the horrified way she'd looked at him... and the way she'd then gotten up and pretended it hadn't happened.

Later, after I'd escaped their house as quickly as I could, then gotten home and felt horribly guilty for leaving her, I'd called her up and insisted that we go to lunch so I could talk to her.

"Lunch," of course, had been code for *I am going to corner you and force you to leave with me.*

And it had gone all right, at first. I'd taken her to her favorite restaurant—not hard when there were only three in that town, and two of them were pretty damn good—and had made small talk about the things I wanted to do with my life now that I found myself back in town without the college degree I'd promised to get.

And then I'd turned the conversation to Roger, and everything had gone sideways on me. She'd been defensive. Angry. Aggressive.

And then, halfway through me practically screaming at her (not really, but you get the idea) about how she owed herself more than that, her eyes had shot over my shoulder to something else, and I'd frozen with that knowledge you get when the person you're talking about is, in fact, standing right behind you.

He had been. And though he hadn't done anything about it right then, the look on his face had promised that he meant to later.

I'd gone home, having failed in my mission to get my mom the hell out of town. And I'd been home for several hours, pacing the apartment and on the phone with my best friend when he got around to calling and making the threat I'd seen promised in his eyes.

I had never in a million years thought I'd be on the other end of a call like the one I got, but when it came right down to it, the whole thing had been... well, pretty simple.

I was on his hit list. Starting right then.

Because I'd dared to try to get my mother out of his clutches, and he had zero intention of letting her go.

He took three sentences to tell me exactly what he meant to do to me if—and when—he saw me again.

I took three minutes to grab the things I thought I couldn't live without and get the hell out of town, with one thought on my mind: I wasn't going to be able to save my mother if I was dead, and from what Roger was saying, me being dead had just moved to the top of his to-do list.

I sighed and leaned my head forward onto the steering wheel of my old Mustang, my mind still trying to grasp the fact that any of this was happening. Because I was from a very, very small town in Minnesota. I'd gone to college in a big city, but I'd gone home to that small town the moment I'd realized that college wasn't for me. I'd never been a bad girl. Always walked the straight line, got the right grades, did the honorable thing.

I had definitely never expected to be caught in the middle of some high-stakes drama where my mom's chain-smoking, wife-beater-wearing, greasy-haired boyfriend called me up and threatened to kill me if he saw me in town again.

"You," I told myself firmly, "have gotten yourself right into the middle of some Hollywood thriller." And not even a good one. This was one of those B-grade movies that used shitty film and even shittier scripts.

"Dammit," I breathed.

Yes, I know what you're already thinking. I should have stuck it out, tried harder to get my mom away from him. I was a terrible daughter for leaving her there alone. A horrible person for thinking of myself instead of her. But the truth was, I already knew what her answer was in terms of getting her out of town, too. I'd seen it in her eyes the moment I brought it up over lunch.

Right before she started shouting at me for trying to interfere with her life.

She might know, somewhere deep in her soul, that he was trouble. She might not be happy or want to stay. But she wasn't in a place where she was ready to admit it yet, and she sure as hell wasn't going to do anything about it.

As far as she was concerned, I was the bad guy for trying to ruin her relationship. So when it came right down to it, I hadn't really had much choice about leaving town—and saving myself—without bringing her along.

Like I said, B-grade film. Shitty script. Impossible situation.

I allowed myself a moment to feel guilty about that and then moved on, realizing that this B-grade actor was fucking starving, and turned to go through the things I'd grabbed before I got the hell out of Dodge. It wasn't much. One large duffle bag, and it was half-empty because I legitimately hadn't known how long I had before Roger the Wife Beater decided to show up at my house rather than just waiting to murder me on the street.

Yes, okay, I heard how dramatic that sounded. But you try being in that situation and tell me how *you'd* react.

A quick paw through the duffle bag told me that I was already low on food. Two bags of chips and a couple of bottles of water. My hand hit the roll of cash I'd also stuffed in the bag, and I felt a thrill of dread go through me.

That wad of cash wasn't nearly as big as I needed it to be.

I didn't have one damn clue what I was going to do in Minneapolis, but I was going to need a lot more money than that if I was going to survive here. The problem was, I didn't want to use my credit cards or debit card. I didn't want to use my cell phone. I didn't want to use anything that might give Roger a way to trace me.

No, I didn't think he was the brightest bulb in the pack. I didn't *really* think he had any contacts with organized crime bosses that would give him high-level capabilities when it came to tracking people when they used their credit cards at hotels or restaurants.

But I didn't know for sure. And that right there was what bothered me.

I didn't know his history or where he'd come from. I didn't know what he did for a living. And as long as that blank space in my knowledge might include "friend of the mob with better connections than anyone realizes," I wasn't going to take any chances.

After all, it would be just like my mother to get involved with someone who was secretly some sort of mafia boss currently in hiding in a small town in Minnesota. She'd done it before.

With my dad.

I grabbed two bills off the roll of cash and climbed out of the car, heading for the convenience store at the end of the alley and already wondering how much I'd be able to buy with $40. I needed stuff that would keep me fed—and last for quite a while—while I started to build a plan for what I was going to do in Minneapolis...

And how I was going to stay safe if Roger was somehow tracing me without me knowing about it.

・・ ⚜ ・・

"ALICE, CONTRARY TO what you believe, this is not my first time in the big city by myself," I said, trying—and failing—to repress a grin.

Hey, I couldn't help it. My best friend, Alice, was a girl I'd known practically since we were in diapers. She'd been by my side through thick and thin, from the first time I got my period to the guy who broke my heart during our senior year, and at this point, she was more of a sister than a friend to me. She was also the girl who'd stayed in our small town when I went away to college.

Which meant she had a very, very odd idea of what "life in the big city" was.

The moment I told her I'd come to Minneapolis to hide out, she'd started worrying that I was in over my head.

"This is your first time in the big city without credit cards or cash, and on your own, with a serial killer after you," she noted.

"Hey, we don't know for sure that he's a serial killer," I told her, still grinning. "He might just be a onetime killer. What's the opposite of serial killer? One-off? Stand-alone?"

"Olivia!" she snapped. "I'm being serious!"

I heard the worry in her voice and turned the snark down several levels. The girl was just trying to take care of me.

"I know, Al. And I'm just trying to make sure I don't find myself in the way when Roger decides he needs a new victim. I'll be fine. I promise."

"Where are you staying? Is there a way I can get a hold of you if I need you?"

I glanced to my right, at the panes of the pay phone booth I'd found outside the convenience store. "Um, not yet," I hedged. "I have a place but there's not exactly a phone."

I could practically hear her glaring at me. "Olivia Jane Cadwell, if you're living in your car and calling that safe enough, I will come to Minneapolis and strangle you."

"You can't," I said. "You don't have a car in which to get here."

"I'll hitchhike," she answered coldly.

The thing was, I totally believed her. Alice Taft was one of the most stubborn people I'd ever known. If she decided that she needed to do something, she'd find a way to do it. No matter how impossible it seemed.

"I'm fine," I told her with more confidence than I actually felt. "I just have to work some things out, and then I'll get you a phone number. I promise."

It wasn't a total lie. I needed to figure out how to get some money—or a job—and then I'd find a place that would accept cash for rent. Without a contract. Or any record that I was staying there.

Maybe some armed guards at the door. Someone to watch my back while I slept.

No problem.

"Okay. If you promise," she said, giving in a lot faster than I'd thought she would.

I promised, then made an excuse about needing to get off the phone—because I had so much I had to do, you know—and hung up. I turned, stepped out of the phone booth and into the now brightly shining sun...

And ran right into the most handsome man I'd ever seen.

I looked up from the rock-hard chest I'd just smashed into and registered very tousled, very expensive brown hair and eyes that looked like a cross between blue and gray. A long, straight nose, incredibly broad cheekbones, a jaw that looked like it could cut glass, and one of those chin dimples.

He looked like he'd stepped right off the cover of a romance novel, all expensive suit and equally expensive cologne.

I opened my mouth to say I was sorry but found that words had evidently become a foreign language.

So instead of saying anything, I turned around and walked as quickly as possible back to my car, stopping only long enough to note that I had another hour on the meter—which meant I could eat and start on a couple of to-do lists before I had to move the car.

As I slid into the back seat, the better to stretch out with my notepad, I let my eyes slide back to the spot where Book Cover Guy had been standing.

He was gone.

And that, I thought, was probably for the best. I was already in enough trouble.

The last thing I needed was some guy deciding he needed to play hero and trying to help.

CHAPTER 3

LEO

WHEN I GOT BACK INTO my building, I got off the elevator on the first floor, walked right to the window, and looked down.

Into the alley that ran between our building and the one next to it.

And there she was. The tiny woman with the dark, wildly curly hair, bright blue eyes, and tendency, evidently, to run right into people on the sidewalk—after coming out of a pay phone booth, of all things—and then walk away without so much as an apology.

I felt my mouth quirk at the thought of her, though. I'd seen the way her eyes had gone wide as she looked up and down my body. And I'd seen the way her mouth had opened on a statement... and then closed when no words presented themselves.

One quick twitch of her right eyebrow, a look that could best have been described as pure sarcasm, and she'd turned and walked away from me like she hadn't just barreled right into my chest and nearly taken me out at the knees.

The even weirder thing was that she'd walked right to a car in the alleyway, checked the meter there, and then gotten into the back seat—along with the large duffle bag she was keeping there. She'd adjusted herself so she was sitting sideways, her legs stretched across the seat, and then she'd started writing something while drinking the soda she'd just bought from the store on the corner.

Yes, I'd stood there and watched her do all this. So what?

Did you miss the part where I said the woman had run right into me at what had to be close to full speed, her eyes on the ground and her mind obviously elsewhere?

Did you also miss the part where I said she was hands down the most gorgeous woman I'd ever seen—if you liked people with far too much hair and eyes that snapped like firecrackers?

Oh, I didn't say that part?

My bad.

She was, hands down, the most intriguing person I thought I'd ever laid eyes on. Short to the point of being almost tiny, incredibly curvaceous, and almost sparking with attitude. She'd taken one look at me, sized me up, and evidently decided that it wasn't worthwhile to speak to me.

It wasn't an experience I had very often. I ran a multibillion-dollar company, and though I didn't like it, I found myself in the public eye relatively often. I was pretty sure the press had actually called me the city's most eligible bachelor several times.

It had been horrifying.

It also meant that almost everyone knew who I was. And when people went out of their way to meet with me or met me in a bar or restaurant, I could very rarely tell whether they were interested in me for myself... or for my money.

You can imagine, I'm sure, how it felt to be bowled over by a girl who looked like she might be five foot five at the most—and then completely written off by her.

I was fascinated.

Even more so when I looked down and saw her get out, check the meter again, and then move the car three spots down to a meter in a spot that had a longer parking option. She got out of the car, filled the meter, and then got back in.

Sliding into the back seat again.

I frowned and tipped my head, wondering at that. She wasn't here to go into any of the buildings around here, or she would have done it. And normal people didn't generally hang out in the back seat of their car.

Normal people also didn't run the meter down and then move to another parking spot to do the same thing over again.

Was she living in her car? In the alleyway next to my building?

Why?

. . . . . .

"LET ME GET THIS STRAIGHT," my best friend, Jack, said over drinks at lunch. "She ran into you, and you were so intrigued by her that you followed her?"

"Not like that," I argued. "You make it sound like I was stalking her or something."

He lifted both eyebrows in a gesture that very clearly said, *If the shoe fits, buddy*.

I shook my head. "I was concerned about her. What kind of person runs right into someone on the street and then doesn't say anything? Just turns and walks the other way like it didn't even happen?"

"Rude ones," he said and popped a fry into his mouth.

I ate one of my own fries, barely tasting the seasoning on it—which was what had made this particular café famous and led to it being our favorite lunch spot—and chewed, my mind going back to everything I'd seen after I got back into my own building.

"The thing is," I said, "about half an hour later, she moved her car up several spots. To a place where she could stay parked for longer."

Jack's eyebrows rose impossibly higher. "So you not only followed her on the street but then went into the building and spied on her? Leo, if you're trying to make me think you're *not* crazy, this is not the way to go about it."

"Okay, now that I'm saying it out loud, it does sound sort of strange," I admitted. "I get it. But I couldn't help it. She's so obviously either lost or living in her car. What was I supposed to do?"

Jack shrugged. "I don't know, count on her to be an adult who can take care of herself and allow her to go on with her life? Without you literally standing above her staring down at her?"

The statement sounded serious. But I could see his lips still wanting to turn up.

And I had to admit that it was all sort of hilarious.

I mean, I didn't even know the girl. I definitely wasn't in the market for any kind of project. And I was most certainly not a knight in shining armor.

What was it to me if she was living in her car, anyhow? If she was, she probably had a very good reason.

One that had nothing to do with me.

I took a bite of my hamburger, turning my mind from the glowing, sparking eyes of a tiny woman who ran into me on the sidewalk and toward the meeting we would be having when we got back to the office—as Jack was my CFO—and started going through the numbers in my head again, trying to figure out whether I'd been missing anything. We were going to talk to the head of my accounting department about why there were some weird numbers coming out of his area of the building, and I wanted to make sure I had everything straight before we met.

I didn't get to be head of such a large company by letting the small mistakes slip through the cracks. If there was something going on in Frederick's department, I wanted to know about it. And I wasn't going to be able to track it down unless I had those numbers right.

. . ⁂ . .

I WAS JUST STEPPING off the curb to cross the street and get back to my building when a car nearly ran me down.

It swerved around me, tires screeching and smoke billowing up around us, and I jumped back, my heart heaving its way right into my mouth and trying to choke me.

Along with the smoke. And the general idea that I'd almost just been hit by a moving vehicle.

I spun to where the car had screeched to a halt and started for the driver's-side door, furious and more than a little bit shocked. What the hell was that car doing driving so fast? This was just an alleyway, for shit's sake!

Then I realized that I recognized the car. And the woman who got out of it.

"I am so sorry!" she said, her eyes down on the sidewalk as she stepped up onto the curb and started toward me. "I didn't see you there, and then you were suddenly there and the only thing I could think was that I was about to kill—"

Her eyes came up to mine, and she jerked to a stop, her sentence cut off mid-apology.

"Oh," she said vaguely. "It's you." Then she remembered what she'd been doing—and saying—and shook her head like she was trying to shake off a bad idea. "I'm so sorry! I definitely didn't expect anyone to come darting out from between two cars just as I was driving by."

I wet my lips, taking in the sparking blue eyes and the wild hair. The curves and the lush lips and porcelain skin and...

Wait. This woman had just nearly run me down. What was I doing cataloging her attributes? I should be shouting at her—and counting my lucky stars that I still had all ten toes.

Instead, I found myself... smiling. Turning my head a bit to give her a flirty look.

"No problem," I said, allowing the smile to go a bit broader. "It's probably my fault. I should obviously have been crossing somewhere else."

She took in the smile, narrowed her eyes a bit, and quirked her eyebrow. "Obviously. I mean, there's a crosswalk right up the street. Anyone who wanted to live to see tomorrow would be using that rather than jaywalking."

I clapped a hand to my chest. "Unfortunately, I've always been a rule breaker. I'm allergic to crosswalks."

"Liar," she returned. "I saw you use one when you were going to the restaurant across the street. Though you had someone else with you at the time. Maybe that was his choice rather than yours."

"It was," I replied quickly. "When I'm with Jack, he makes me follow the rules. I hate it."

She snorted at that and then let herself go and gave me a full-on giggle.

Followed by a growl from her midsection.

She clapped a hand over her stomach, her fair face going incredibly red, and started to turn away. "Sorry, I've got to go. I—"

I caught her arm before she could go far, my body acting without my brain's instructions and leaving my brain to catch up with words.

"Where are you going?" I asked quickly. "You're obviously hungry. Come have some lunch with me."

She shot a cool, amused glance over her shoulder. "Buddy, I literally just saw you go to lunch with someone else. That line's not going to work with me, I'm afraid."

I shrugged. "You just almost hit me with your car. I'm thinking the least you can do is have lunch with me to make up for it. What do you say?"

Her eyes narrowed in what I already thought of as her thinking gaze. And her stomach rumbled again—at which point she rolled those eyes and gave in.

"Lunch and you won't sue me for almost hitting you?" she asked.

"I swear it on my mother's lemon cake," I told her solemnly.

This received another eyebrow quirk. "I've never had her cake. I don't even know if that's a valid swear."

I looped her arm through mine and started walking back toward the restaurant I'd just come from, where they had the best burgers and fries in the entire city. "I'll bring you her cake tomorrow, and then you'll see just how serious that swear is."

I didn't think about the fact that I'd just promised to bring her cake tomorrow. I didn't think about the fact that she was a total stranger who was evidently living in her car outside of my office.

I didn't think about who she was or what she might be doing there or why the hell I'd thought it was a good idea to promise her a slice of my mother's cake.

I was too busy thinking about the way her eyes had sparkled at me when she laughed... and how my skin was buzzing at having her tucked into my side like she belonged there.

· · ~§~ · ·

"LEO," THE HOSTESS SAID, surprised. "Am I imagining things, or were you already here once today?"

"About half an hour ago?" I asked. "Wasn't me. That's the guy I'm hiring to stand in for me when I don't want to make personal appearances. It works well, doesn't it?"

She gave me the grin I knew she would—after all, I was the rich guy who ate here every day and probably paid for her entire salary all on my own—and turned her eyes to the woman on my arm.

Her brows came down a bit, and I knew why that was. The girl—whose name I still didn't even know—didn't look like someone I'd normally be seen with. She was small and dressed in nothing more than jeans and a T-shirt. Her hair was wild, and she didn't have a stitch of makeup on.

She looked, in short, like she'd come from the country and then slept in her car.

And I couldn't wait to get her story out of her.

"Two," I told the hostess simply. "A booth, please. Near the window."

Her eyes came back to me, and she nodded like this happened all the time. Then she turned and walked toward the booth I'd requested, her shoulders stiff.

Snob, I thought. She was a hostess in a bar and grill. What was she doing judging the girl at my side?

The same thing everyone else in this city did, I realized. Judging my life like it was available for public consumption.

Just like Meghan had told me they did.

She'd also told me that I needed to start dating a single girl to make the public think I was more stable and to please the board. Well, I was out on a date with a girl in the middle of the day at a normal place.

True, I didn't think the tousled, creased, and nameless girl next to me was probably what Meghan had had in mind when she'd given me that lecture.

But I found that I didn't much care about that.

I was too busy thinking up questions for the nameless girl—and trying to guess at how she'd answer them.

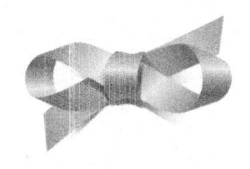

CHAPTER 4

LEO

"SO," SHE SAID THE MOMENT we slid into the booth. "Leo, huh? Like the astrological sign?"

"I suppose so," I said. "Though I'm a Taurus."

She stuck her hand out to shake. "Nice to meet you, Leo. Olivia. Gemini/Cancer."

I frowned. "How did you get two signs? Is there a sign-up sheet for that? Because I'd like to add Scorpio to my list, if I can."

She shook her head. "Not possible. Scorpio and Taurus are too far apart. You can only have two if they're close enough together. I was born on the cusp of Gemini and Cancer. The in-between, where one is ending and the other is starting. Which means I have two signs. Three personalities."

"Wait, three?"

I was already starting to think this girl was going to be harder to keep up with than I'd realized.

"Three. Two for Gemini—the twins—and one for Cancer. I mean, two for Cancer, if you want to get really picky, since there's the public side and the private side." She paused and looked at me, eyes large. And she must have seen exactly how much I was already starting to doubt her sanity, because she started giggling. "I'm only kidding. I only have one personality. Two, max. On a bad day."

I waited, wondering if she was still kidding or if this was the truth.

She noticed me waiting and widened her own eyes. "Did you *want* me to have four personalities or something?"

Okay, not kidding. Two personalities, check.

"Not at all," I told her quickly. "Two is quite enough, I think."

Holly, the waitress who had served Jack and me about an hour ago, arrived at the table at that moment, her eyebrows raised. "Hey, Leo. Is it me, or were you literally just here?"

"I was just here," I confirmed. Then my gaze met Olivia's... and registered the lifting of one of her eyebrows as she asked the question Holly hadn't.

What the hell was I doing back here?

The thing was, I didn't *really* know the answer.

"I ran into someone who needed lunch and volunteered to procure it for her," I said, turning back to Holly. "I'll take a beer. Can you bring a menu for..." I glanced at Olivia again, wondering if this was even okay with her.

I mean, I'd basically just kidnapped her and forced her into a restaurant. Now I was forcing a menu on her.

And I didn't even know her.

A quirk of her lips told me that she was just fine with the situation, though, and I continued my statement to Holly.

"Menu for her, drink for me," I finished. "Please."

She nodded quickly. "Your usual?"

"Of course," I told her with a smile.

I trusted her to bring me exactly what I wanted. I ate here often enough—with Holly as the waitress—for her to know what I generally ordered.

Once she disappeared, I turned back to my lunch date.

I wanted to ask her if she was in fact living in her car. Like, that was the only thing I could think of.

But something told me it wouldn't be popular, and I didn't want to piss any of her personalities off.

"So, Olivia. What do you do when you're not trying to hit random pedestrians in alleyways?"

"Well, Leo, when people aren't randomly walking out in front of me in alleyways, I'm generally quite a good driver," she answered quickly, her face straight.

Then she stared at me like that was all she was going to give me.

"So... you just spend all your time driving around, being a good driver?" I prodded. "Or do you have a life outside of that?"

It was meant to be a joke, but the shadow that crossed her face—and stuck—told me that it definitely wasn't funny.

I saw her make the decision to put the shadow away, though, and a moment later, she was leaning forward, all coy flirtiness.

"Well, I'm not supposed to say this, because, you know, top secret shit, but I'm actually a mutant. Superhero powers."

I leaned forward as well, trying very, very hard not to laugh at a woman who could come up with a story like that on such short notice. "Really? What's the going rate for superheroes? Do you work on an hourly charge?"

She shrugged casually. "I'm not at liberty to say, I'm afraid. I'm currently contracted to the CIA, and my contract is pretty strict."

At that, I did start laughing, mostly because I just couldn't help myself.

Holly brought the menu and my beer then, and Olivia quickly ordered half the things on the menu—at which point I reminded myself that this woman appeared to have been living in her car. which meant, I assumed, that she was also living without anything even remotely resembling warm food.

How long had she been in that situation? And what had put her there? Didn't she have a regular home? A job?

People she belonged to?

I forced my mind to let go of the questions, knowing instinctively that she didn't want to talk about whatever the answers were, and started talking about myself, instead. And before I knew it, I was telling her about growing up the oldest child in a household where both of my parents worked so much that I only got to see them on weekends.

Spending more time with my books than my parents.

Learning to run a business at fourteen, when my father suddenly fell ill and couldn't do as much as he once had. And eventually taking that business over.

And becoming the carbon copy of what my dad had been—without the family. I worked just as hard as him and had built the company up to twice as large as he had.

I'd also never found anyone to share my rare days off with.

"Which means you're just as lonely now as you were when you were a kid," Olivia concluded quietly.

I started, having forgotten that I was saying all of those things out loud, and then frowned. "I'm not sure I'd put it quite that way," I said. "I'm closer to my brothers now than I was when we were young, and I've got friends. I'm not exactly... lonely."

Or at least I had never thought I was before.

Once she'd said it, though, I couldn't get it out of my head. I couldn't get around how true it was.

I couldn't stop wondering how many other people had thought the same thing... and been too afraid to say it out loud.

One more thing Olivia had done to make herself stand out from the crowd. And I hadn't even really known her for more than an hour yet.

. . ~ . .

I WALKED HER TO HER car after lunch, feeling incredibly torn about just... leaving her there, and stopped her right before she ducked into it.

"Do you have a number I could call you at?" I asked, my fingers curved around her bicep. "Some way I could get in touch with you?"

She looked at me like I was losing my mind. "Why, so I can come by to try to hit you with my car again?"

"Maybe I like that sort of attention," I said, realizing now that I didn't have any reason for actually wanting to talk to her again, aside from just... wanting to talk to her again.

I didn't really think she was going to accept that as an adequate reason, though.

She snorted. "Yeah, right. You, with your thousand-dollar suit and even more expensive haircut? I bet you usually travel with armed guards who make sure the street is clear when you cross it."

I leaned toward her and dropped my voice. "So you can understand, then, why it's so exciting to be out here on my own, nearly getting run over by beautiful women."

She blushed deeply at that—as I'd hoped she would—and cast a look up at me through her lashes. "I don't have a phone on me right now. But I can make arrangements to be around again if it's that important."

And with that, she turned, got into her car, and skidded out of the parking place, kicking up gravel and dust in her wake like some heroine in a movie.

I watched her go, still caught on her vague promise to be around, and then shook myself and headed for the office.

I had to admit that I'd probably never see the girl again. She was living in her car in an alley in Minneapolis, didn't carry a phone, and hadn't even given me her full name.

Lunch might have been fun. That didn't mean she was going to show up again.

Still.

I sort of hoped she did.

· · ～ · ·

"I THINK SHE'S LIVING in her car," I said, staring through the window at the place where she'd been parked when I dropped her off.

Jack snorted. "And you care because...?"

I glanced at him, surprised and very disillusioned at the question. "You don't think it's awful for someone to just be living in their car in an alley by themselves?"

He just smirked. "Do you think it would be better if she had company?"

There were times when I really questioned why I kept this guy as my best friend. "I think it would be better if she wasn't living in the alley at all. Or in her car. I think it would be better if she actually had a home."

When I looked at Jack again, I saw that the jokester was gone, replaced by the stern, serious man I normally saw only when we were in the office or I was in some sort of trouble.

The version of Jack who had rescued me when I got in over my head in college. Or fell and broke my leg that one time we'd tried cliff diving.

The version I knew I could count on.

"So do something about it," Serious Jack said.

It caught me so off guard that my brain went skidding to a halt at his words. "Huh?"

He rolled his eyes. "There are days, Leo, when I really wonder how you run a company like this. If you don't like that she's living on the street, in her car, then do something about it. You're a billionaire with more homes than you can use. Hell, I don't know if some of those homes have ever even been *slept* in. Give her a place to stay. Get her off the streets if it bothers you so much. You're the one who's constantly giving to charity. Practice it in real life."

I realized at that moment that my mouth was actually hanging open at his words and snapped it shut.

He was right. I had several homes in the city and several outside of it. A couple in other states.

I really only used the penthouse in Minneapolis.

Jack was also right in that I could loan her any one of those homes. If I trusted her not to screw them up. If she trusted me enough to stay in one of my houses.

It was the ideal solution.

Except I had an even better one.

She needed a place to stay and three warm meals a day—or at least I was guessing she needed something like that. At the very least, she was probably tired of sitting in her car all the time.

I had recently found out that I needed to improve my public persona. I evidently, according to Meghan, needed to make several appearances with the same woman on my arm. And she'd even given me a specific target: the large charity auction the city was having next week.

A woman who needed a place to stay. A man who needed a favor that involved a woman pretending to date him.

If I hadn't known any better, I would have said it was fate.

Only I didn't believe in fate. Or astrological signs.

That sort of thing seemed to be way more up Olivia's alley. So to speak.

CHAPTER 5

OLIVIA

I BIT MY LIP, THINKING through the steps of the plan I was cobbling together, and then bent and scratched more of it out in my notebook.

Then I stared at it, feeling sort of... even more hopeless than I had before I started building the plan. Four points so far. Four options for trying to find a job while living in my car and not having access to important things like running water and a hair dryer.

Not that a hair dryer was really that useful when you had hair that curled like it was possessed by a local demon. But with certain attachments, it worked.

And it was definitely an important part of making myself presentable for things like job interviews.

Other things I was currently lacking: access to the internet. Access to a working phone number. Any leads whatsoever.

Overall, things weren't looking great. It was my second day of living in the car, and though I'd so far succeeded in avoiding detection by Roger and whatever minions he might have on the case—or at least, I thought he had—this scene was definitely starting to get old.

I frowned and rewound that thought. I *thought* I'd been able to avoid detection when it came to Roger.

But I couldn't know that for sure.

I'd taken off in the middle of the night, counting on the cover of darkness and the element of surprise to protect me from my mother's boyfriend. But what if he'd been having my house watched or something? What if they'd been tailing me, one of those anonymous sets of lights in the darkness on my way to Minneapolis?

What if they were in one of the cars that continually drove down this alley with the conveniently lax parking rules?

What if they were parked here right now?

My eyes shot to the rearview mirror, and I met my own gaze, horrified at this thought. No, I didn't know if Roger was actually going to do anything. Great cats, I didn't even know if he was anything more than just a bully who didn't like being called on his shit.

But if he was more than just a bully and he actually did intend to do something about the fact that I'd called him out, then I was a freaking idiot to think that changing locales had been enough to throw him off my scent—especially when I'd literally left the town where he was currently living.

Shit, I was stupid. Shit, I was ignorant.

And then I'd come to Minneapolis and made a fucking spectacle of myself by staying in the same place—in my car!—for two days straight.

Taking an entire hour out of my day to actually go out in public with a guy that definitely had to be one of the most eligible bachelors in the entire fucking state. Flirting with him like nothing else mattered. Making jokes.

Laughing.

Allowing myself to feel entirely too safe, just because I was with a guy who exuded confidence and security.

I turned and scanned the street behind me—and all the cars parked there—for... something. I didn't even know what I was looking for. There was no one there, though, and I whirled back around in my seat, reaching for the keys.

I needed to move. I needed to find a new place to hang out. I could go back to figuring out how to get a job once I knew I was in a less predictable location.

I'd got the keys into the ignition and was starting to turn them when someone banged on the window right next to my ear.

I jumped as far as the seat belt would let me and jerked away from the window, a scream on my lips and my eyes on the glass.

And then I saw that it wasn't Roger or any other goon standing out there on the sidewalk. It was Leo, the guy I had lunch with yesterday.

He of the insanely sharp jaw, dimpled chin, and shocking eyes.

I rolled the window down, trying really hard to control my breathing—and my heart—and scowled at him.

"Do you have any idea how rude it is to sneak up on someone like that?" I asked, forcing my voice to go lighter than it wanted to.

I threw a smile in, just to make it even gentler. I mean, it wasn't going to do me any good to alienate the one cool person I'd met in the city so far.

"It is bad manners, I'll admit that much," he said, nodding and looking unfairly handsome. "But I think you're going to forgive me when you hear why I did it."

"That's an awfully big presumption. I don't generally forgive people who try to scare the shit out of me."

He cocked his head like he wasn't used to people refusing him—which, let's face it, he probably wasn't. I didn't know who he was or what his position was in life, but it didn't take a lot to guess that he was important.

His shoes probably cost more than a full month of rent on my apartment. The guy was practically bleeding wealth through his pores.

People like that didn't usually hear the word "no" often.

Which sort of made it even more surprising that he was bothering with me.

Which made me even more suspicious.

"But," he said, all charm and chin dimple, "I have a very good proposition for you."

I pressed my lips together. A proposition, eh? I didn't usually entertain those.

I also wasn't really in a position to turn anything down.

"Step into my office," I said slowly, gesturing to my passenger seat.

Leo went quickly around the front of the car while I did my level best to speed clean the passenger seat, which had become my storage area for things like to-do lists and candy bar wrappers. I grabbed the last wrapper and the biggest notebook out of the seat just in time for him to pull the door open and slide in.

He looked around, looking... impressed.

"This is quite a restoration job," he said, his voice holding more than a little bit of awe. "What is this, a '69?"

"It's a '67, actually. Mustang Shelby. Fully restored."

He whistled slowly. "Sharp. And red. I like it. All sports cars should be red."

"Totally agree," I said, feeling myself start to melt a little. "Unless it's a Ferrari, in which case yellow is a completely valid replacement."

He shot me a look out of the corner of his eye. "Debatable," he said shortly.

I grinned. "I'd be fully willing to debate you on that point. Now, my awesome car aside, what's this proposition?"

He actually turned to face me in the car, which I wouldn't have believed possible for such a tall man. But the guy was evidently insanely flexible.

His eyes, however, were not. They were convinced. Steady.

Not ready to accept no for an answer. Or at least... No, I thought, amending my impression. It wasn't that he wasn't going to accept a refusal. It was that he was absolutely, totally, 100 percent convinced that he was doing the right thing.

And that realization told me more about his character than our entire lunch yesterday had done.

He was one of the good guys. One of the guys who thought he could save the world—and didn't see any reason not to follow through on that.

I hadn't known many people like that. In fact, my life was sadly lacking in white knights.

Whatever he was about to tell me, I thought, was something I needed to actually listen to. If this guy actually wanted to help me, then I needed to get past my usually stubborn nature and give it a chance.

"Well?" I asked, seeing that his mouth was still closed, his proposition still unsaid. "Are you going to let me in on the secret, or do you expect me to say yes just on principle?"

His lips twitched.

"Would you tell me yes before you knew what the deal was?"

"Absolutely not. I don't even trust my best friend enough for that."

His brow crimped at that, like he wanted to ask what exactly I meant, but he cleared the look and jumped to the point of the entire meeting.

"I can't help but notice that you're spending a whole lot of time in your car, and that you're not from Minneapolis," he said smoothly. "And I'm guessing that means that you're probably tired of spending time in your car. Maybe even looking for a different place to sleep."

I kept my mouth shut. Mostly because I didn't know how to respond to someone who had—correctly—guessed that I was currently living in my car.

"The thing is," he continued in my silence, "I think I might have an answer to your predicament. I want to give you a place to live, for at least a little while. And a job."

My mind jerked to a stop at his words, and for a second, all I could think about was that he was offering a place to stay. A roof. A kitchen.

A shower. With hot water—which would be miles better than the bathroom sink at the convenience store on the corner, which was where I'd been washing my hair in the morning.

Safety.

And then my mind started moving again, and I put the other pieces together.

"I'm not a prostitute," I told him sharply.

He laughed. "Honestly, that idea never even crossed my mind," he said. "I need—"

"Let me guess. Arm candy."

Shit, that was so cliché. So freaking predictable that it almost made me gag.

But I didn't. Because I was already starting to get attached to the idea of that hot water.

"Why is it rich guys like you never have girls around when they need them?" I asked, confused. "You're rich. You're at least relatively good-looking. You obviously know cars. And I'm guessing you must have girls hanging off you. So why the hell would you need to go outside of your circle—to the alley outside of your building—to look for a girl?"

He grimaced. "First, I do not have girls hanging off me. Second, you would be surprised at how difficult it is for someone like me to socialize with a woman without her..."

"Ah," I interrupted again. "Without her having ulterior motives."

He gave me a grin of appreciation. "Exactly. I couldn't have put it better myself."

"It makes sense," I said slowly, thinking through it as I spoke. "You're a rich, successful guy. And I'm guessing most of the women your friends know are looking for rich, successful guys to tie down."

"And I am most certainly not interested in being tied down," he confirmed, nodding. Then he tipped his head and gave me an intense look. "It's really, really weird to be speaking about this so frankly."

I just shrugged. "I've never been good at beating around the bush. I'm a numbers girl. Emotions and manipulation don't come easy for me. So what's your deal? I act as your arm candy and you...?"

He nodded. "I give you a place to stay for however long you want to stay there. Food. And a salary."

It was like I'd fallen into some kind of weird, fucked-up fairy tale. I act like this guy's date for a week or two and I get a place to stay and food. A salary, no less.

Stay two weeks and then get the hell out of there with cash in my pocket for a hotel room, I thought practically. Get out of my car. Off the streets.

And into a place where I might actually be able to do some serious planning.

"Hot water and as many baths as I want?" I asked. "A room of my own? And some clothes?"

Yes, it sounded materialistic, but I wanted the terms straight before I agreed to anything.

"Done, done, and done. And anything else you need in the meantime. In exchange for you making yourself available and playing nice when I need you to."

"Done," I replied quickly.

I stuck my hand out to shake on it, repressed the shiver it gave me when his hand engulfed mine, and quickly rearranged my idea of what the next few days would look like.

"When do we head home?"

He shook my hand firmly, seeming like he definitely wasn't experiencing the lightning bolts that were currently shooting through *my* body, and nodded once.

"Half an hour. Let me close up my office and let my assistant know I'm leaving for the rest of the day. You stay here."

He was gone before I could answer him—or say anything about him already ordering me around.

Honestly, he wouldn't have needed to tell me to stay there. He'd just promised me the very thing I'd known I needed.

Security. Safety.

Yeah, it was slightly weird to be going to some guy's house to stay there and play his girlfriend.

But I'd have a roof over my head without having to use my real name, which would make me untraceable. It would get me off the streets, which would make me more secure. And if Leo's appearance was any indication, whatever building he was living in was going to come pre-fitted with security and probably an alarm.

Which meant that even if Roger was somehow following me, he wouldn't be able to get in.

For two weeks, at least, I wasn't going to have to worry about my mother's boyfriend tracking me down.

Bonus: I'd be living with the sexiest man I'd ever set eyes on. And there was absolutely nothing wrong with that, either.

CHAPTER 6

LEO

THE MOMENT MY EYES opened, I started grinning.

Olivia was in the shower in the bathroom in her suite, and that simple idea made me feel... weirdly complete. Or... No, not complete, but...

Something. Something that was the opposite of lonely.

Full, in a way that I couldn't really explain.

My grin got bigger, and I went through last night very quickly in my mind. She'd started staring the moment I got her into the penthouse—courtesy of the elevator that opened right onto what was essentially my floor—and hadn't stopped.

I mean, she hadn't stopped at all. Her mouth had dropped open when we got off the elevator and had stayed that way as I walked her through the living room and library—both done in classic furniture and old-fashioned wood paneling—and gave her a tour of the kitchen, which was no more modern in appearance, though the appliances were all top-of-the-line.

What can I say? I had a thing for classic looks. I might live in the most expensive penthouse in the city. That didn't mean I wanted boring, ultra-modern furniture in grays and reds.

I was way too attached to deep carpets, rich leather, and cushy couches.

I'd watched Olivia take it all in, her jaw hanging open, and then do a double take at the number of books lining the walls of my library.

I'd taken her to the guest suite, told her that the entire set of rooms was hers to do with as she would, and left her with the promise that the bathtub in the bathroom was larger than any two tubs I'd ever seen before and was at her disposal.

The last I'd seen of her, she'd been heading for that very tub, her shoes already off and her hands tangled in her curls as she pulled them off her neck.

I bit my lip at that memory, my mind going a bit further into the bathroom with her than I actually did, and then promptly put the thought away.

Yes, she was a tiny, curvaceous, and entirely mysterious woman. Beautiful and somehow more interesting than any girl I'd ever met before. Incredibly alluring.

Unbelievably sexy.

And none of that mattered at all. Because she was also my guest, and that meant that I wasn't going to lay one single hand on her.

That wasn't our deal. Our deal was a roof over her head in exchange for her being my shield against the press. There was no room there for me thinking she was sexy.

There was definitely no room for me imagining what she looked like underneath those clothes.

· · ⚜ · ·

I WAS POURING MYSELF a cup of coffee when Olivia emerged from her bedroom, dressed in a slightly different version of the same outfit she'd been in yesterday. She did look well rested, at least, the dark circles gone from under her eyes and the lines of tension around her mouth smoothed out.

She also looked very clean, given the fact that her hair was still soaking wet.

"Enjoying the hot water?" I asked, fighting to keep my face straight.

She rolled her eyes to the ceiling. "You wouldn't believe how much I'm enjoying it. Besides, you told me I could use as much of it as I wanted."

"True. I'm glad to see you're taking advantage of that. Might be the best deal I've ever made."

She let her eyes rove up and down my body, her face taking on a cocky, very stubborn slant. "Well, don't think that means I'm easy to please. Because I'm definitely not. I'll need more than just hot water to keep me happy. Starting with coffee. Very hot coffee. Preferably with mocha in it."

I slapped a hand to my chest. "My house is your house. Help yourself."

She moved more quickly for the coffee maker than I would have thought possible, and before long, she was actually rifling through my cupboards, checking out what I might have in there.

"No mocha," she grumbled. "But I see you're a big fan of bagels and cream cheese."

She was, in fact, currently spreading a very generous layer of cream cheese across an untoasted bagel. When she noticed me noticing her doing it, she grinned, totally unrepentant.

"Hope you don't mind if I have one."

"My house, your house, remember? Help yourself."

"Your house, my house only for the next week," she said firmly. "Until you have your fancy shindig. Then I'm going to be on my way to the next big thing."

I stopped myself in the midst of saying what I'd been about to say, which was that she could run down to the market if there was anything else she wanted and should feel free to use the account I had there from here on out, and shut my mouth.

Right. Only for a week. I'd thought the deal we made was for slightly longer than that, but I wasn't going to argue with her about it.

"One week of your time, and then I shall free you," I agreed. "Heaven forbid I force you to stay in this place any longer than you want to."

She took a bite of the bagel and grinned around it. "Heaven forbid. Don't you have to go to work or something?"

I did. I didn't want to—the idea of her being in my house was far too new, far too exciting for me to think I could focus on being in the office—but the company wasn't going to run itself.

"I do," I told her. "Are you... going to be here?"

It sounded weird. Even as I said it, I knew it sounded weird. I sounded too off-balance, too questioning.

I sounded like I didn't know how to talk to another human being—which had, to be honest, never been a problem before.

Why the hell was it a problem now? It wasn't like Olivia had any special powers or anything. She was just a girl. Who I happened to have picked up off the street.

Who was going to be living in my house for the next week or so.

She shrugged, blowing right past the awkwardness of my question, and I wondered if that was because she was being kind or if she actually hadn't been paying that much attention to what I was saying.

Probably the latter. This girl had no reason to be kind to me. She barely even knew me.

"This might be a surprise to you, but I don't actually have a lot of friends in Minneapolis. No one to go out with. So yes to the staying here."

I saw the opening and jumped on it, leaning my hands on the counter and moving forward a bit. "You don't have friends here? What are you doing here, then?"

That shadow crossed her face again, and I saw her expression, which had been at least trying to move toward open friendliness, shutter and snap shut. "Can't tell you," she quipped, her voice too high. "Superhero with a government contract, remember?"

"Right," I said, not believing a word of it. "My mistake."

I gave her a quick grin, then told her I'd see her later, turned, and made my way to the door, realizing now—too late—that I was going to have a complete stranger staying in my house for the entire day, doing who knew what.

I'd have to tell Timothy, the doorman, to keep an eye on things up here. Call me if he saw anyone making their way through the lobby with my favorite chair in tow.

• • ⚜ • •

AS IT TURNED OUT, THINKING about Olivia being in my house didn't just disappear when I got to the office.

I was, in fact, dreaming about it—or at least thinking about it—when Jonathan, head of the accounting department, walked into my office directly after lunch.

"Jonathan," I said, surprised at his visit. I dealt with the man relatively often, but only when we had a meeting scheduled to go over the company's numbers. Generally, he met with Jack, who was CFO, and Jack passed any information I might need on to me.

Come to think of it, I wasn't sure Jonathan had ever come into my office without a direct invitation.

"Do you need something?" I asked, frowning. "Going to turn Jack in for running the department badly?"

He chuckled and shook his head. "You and I both know that if the department was running badly, it would be my fault and not Jack's. Even if Jack was responsible, he'd find a way to charm his way out of it. Pin it on me."

"That," I told him, "is exactly true. And he's always been that way. Ever since we were little kids. Always talked me into things I knew we shouldn't do and, when we got caught, managed to make whatever adult had caught us think that it had actually been my idea rather than his." I paused and thought about it for a moment. "Honestly, it's a shock that I kept him around as long as I have."

"You kept him around because he's good at his job," Jonathan said with another smile. "That whole best-friend thing probably helps, though."

"It probably does," I admitted. "But enough about him. What's up?"

He bit his lip, looked unsure for a second, and then walked toward my desk, ending the stroll by sliding a piece of paper onto my desk.

I looked down quickly, confused, and read the first line of the text. *I, Jonathan Smith, am submitting my resignation from the role of...*

My eyes shot back up to Jonathan, who was looking incredibly guilty.

"Resignation?" I gasped.

This was the guy who kept the accounting department running. Sure, Jack was in charge of it in name, but he didn't really do that much when it came to the day-to-day operations. He was an executive.

Jonathan was the one in the trenches.

He grimaced. "I know, and I'm sorry. It's not where I saw this going, either. But Sally is on the edge of retirement, and she's got this idea about a year off to tour the world. I can't exactly let her go on her own."

"Who would?" I asked. "A tour of the world! You'd have to be pretty stupid to let her leave you behind. I mean, just imagine all the men she'll meet in Italy."

"And Spain. And France," he agreed.

I took the paper and slid it toward me, glancing through the rest of the text. He'd given us two weeks, at least.

It wasn't much. But it was better than nothing.

"Have you tried reminding her that just because she's getting that early retirement doesn't mean you are?" I asked, my eyes still on the paper.

"I tried. She responded with the reminder that we aren't getting any younger, and we don't get a restart at the end of this life."

I felt my lips curve. Sally Smith had always been incredibly charming... and overly straightforward. "That sounds like her. And in a vacuum, I'd agree with her. But this..."

"Leaves you in a tough spot. I know. That's why I'm going to make it my mission to find my replacement before I leave. I know you don't have time for it, and let's face it: if we let Jack do the search, he'll end up with the first beautiful woman who compliments his shoes."

I burst out in laughter at that. Because it was definitely true.

"Find the person and train them?" I asked, trying to negotiate as much as I could out of what was going to be a disaster for the division—and, if it went badly, for the company itself.

"Find them and train them," he said with a nod. "I won't let Sally book our first flight until I'm satisfied that you're going to be okay."

I sighed... but I was already moving forward. Starting to plan for how we were going to fix this.

"Well, I know Sally well enough to know that if she's made up her mind, nothing I can say or offer will change it. If you can help us with the search and training, that's all I can ask of you, I suppose."

Jonathan said something generic about how great it had been to work for the company and how much he didn't want to leave—which was rich, considering he was in fact leaving—and then turned and left, mumbling something about getting started with the search.

I watched him go, my mind flipping through my mental Rolodex as I tried to fill the spot he was going to leave open.

This company netted billions every year, and Jonathan had been in charge of making sure those billions were tracked and taken care of. We weren't going to last long without someone in that position.

This was very, very bad.

I was still eyeing the door and thinking about it when it swung open again, this time admitting Meghan.

"Right now?' I asked. "What are you guys doing out there, standing in line to come in and deliver bad news?"

She looked shocked. "When have I ever brought you bad news? It's my job to keep bad news from happening!"

I groaned at that, which was definitely a glossy version of her job description. "And yet the last time you were in here, just a few days ago, you were chock-full of bad news."

She made a face at me. "I was in here to try to keep you from making the news any worse. And I'm in here now to follow up on that. What do you have for me, Leo? Please tell me it's something good."

I gave another internal groan, cursing the world about the need for publicists—and then cursing the world for the existence of the press itself—and then dove in.

"Actually, I do have something for you," I said grudgingly. "I'm dating a woman, and she's going to come with me to the charity auction. She's smart. She's beautiful. I think even you will approve of her."

Meghan whipped out her ever-present binder and started jotting things down in it, no doubt cooking up some new form of magic with the details I was giving her.

"This is terrific," she muttered. When she looked up, her eyes were shining. "What's her name? Where'd you meet her?"

I grinned despite myself. "Her name's Olivia, and I met her in the alley right outside the building. When she almost ran me over."

"Solid. Gold," she murmured, writing feverishly.

She turned and left the room without even looking my way again, which was a small blessing unto itself.

Of course, it left me sitting in my office on my own, with Olivia once more on my mind.

She was going to need clothes if we were going to pull this off, I realized. Plus, I was pretty sure clothes were part of the deal I'd made with her.

I reached for the phone, intent on dialing my assistant for help in that regard.

And while I had her on the phone, I was going to ask about dinner reservations for Olivia and me. This was going to be our first night as a couple.

Surely I should take her out to dinner to celebrate the landmark.

Right?

Or was that too much? Laying it on too thick? Being presumptive? Shit. Maybe I should ask Janice about that as well.

CHAPTER 7

OLIVIA

I SPENT MY DAY GOING through the library with a fine-toothed comb.

I mean, that's not *all* I did. Obviously. But it was definitely the *first* thing I did. After I finished another three bagels—one with peanut butter smeared across it instead of cream cheese.

Hey, don't look at me that way. If you'd spent two days living in your car and surviving on potato chips, beef jerky, and soda, and you suddenly had access to a kitchen with a toaster and all the bagels you could eat (evidently Leo really, *really* liked them), you would have done the same.

You legitimately don't realize how amazing hot food is until it becomes hard to come by.

I'd stuffed the last bite in my mouth, grabbed my cup of coffee (I'd taken the liberty of making three additional pots since Leo left), made a mental note to ask Leo what it was between him and bagels, and then headed for the library we'd passed through on our way into the house.

It was kind of a weird place to put it, I thought. Right in the room where anyone else would have put the living room. Definitely the largest room in the entire place.

Then again, if one really loved books—which it definitely looked like he did—then I guessed the biggest room in the house was the logical place for the library.

I had to admit, as I walked in, that the place was fucking gorgeous. When we'd come up to the penthouse—on an elevator that opened up right into his own foyer, if you please—I'd been sure we were about to enter one of those truly atrocious apartments where the artwork makes zero sense and the furniture is all done in reds, blacks, and whites, and completely uncomfortable.

Instead, I'd found a home that consisted of dark wood, lots of leather, and chairs so comfortable that I wanted to sit down in one, grab a book, and spend the rest of the day just resting.

Plus, a kitchen full of bagels and cream cheese. A guest suite that had been done in linens so nice that I'd almost had an orgasm over them. A full bathroom to myself.

This Leo guy was really starting to grow on me, and that didn't happen often. Honestly, for the most part, I didn't like people all that much.

So meeting a guy by mistake, and then saying yes to his crazy idea about me living with him and pretending to be his arm candy for a week... and then finding out that I actually sort of *liked* him?

This was definitely one of the weirdest experiences of my entire life.

I mean, when you thought about it, it was just a logical follow-up to having to run away from my hometown because my mother's crazy boyfriend actually threatened my life for calling him out on his shit.

Living in my car for two full days, too afraid to check in to a hotel because it would mean using my credit cards.

Throwing my cell phone out the window as I tore away from my hometown.

Leaving most of my belongings—and my best friend—behind me.

Yep, just your normal, run-of-the-mill weekend for yours truly.

Honestly, not even running away from home to go to college in NYC had been this exciting.

I stifled a totally irrational giggle at the thought and turned toward the overstuffed shelves of the library, stepping toward the first one and lifting my hand up to gently run my finger along the spines. Then I tilted my head, frowned, and ran my finger back along the spines I'd just touched.

Was that...?

It couldn't be.

I very gently pulled the book in question out of the row it was sitting in and opened it up to the rights page.

It was.

I was holding a first-edition (American) copy of *Wuthering Heights* by Emily Brontë. And next to it, early editions of *Jane Eyre* and *Pride and Prejudice*. When I stepped back and looked at the entire row, I saw that those weren't the only ones, either. The guy had Poe, Twain, and every poet known to man—or at least every poet known to this woman.

All in early editions. All in protective wrapping that would, I assumed, keep the covers pristine. Or at least as pristine as they had been when Leo acquired them.

I took a step back from that shelf, suddenly terrified that I'd actually touched books that had to be worth thousands of dollars, and looked for shelves that were a little bit more my speed.

It didn't take me long to find them. On the other side of the room, I found what I thought of as his "trade" shelves, packed full of more common, garden-variety authors and books that had been published within the last decade. And boy, did the man have a collection. There had to be thousands of books in here. Well... maybe hundreds.

Either way, there were a lot.

"Must be nice to be so rich you can just buy whatever you see, regardless of whether you mean to read it," I muttered, pulling a thriller that looked like it had never even been cracked open off the shelf. I grabbed a couple more—all equally new-looking—swore to myself that they'd look just as good when I put them back, and then made my way to the reading nook I'd already decided was my favorite, which consisted of two enormous armchairs, a fairly plain little table that made up for it with the gorgeous wood it was made of, and a window set into the wall for light.

There was a lamp, too, but the window was so perfect that I didn't think I'd have to turn the thing on.

I settled into the chair, grinning to myself and more content than I had been in years, and opened the first book.

Coffee, brand-new books, and a reading nook. Could life get any sweeter?

The fact that Roger and his (possibly imaginary) goons didn't have the first clue I was here just made the whole thing even better.

. . ❧ . .

I JUMPED ABOUT A MILE off the chair when the doorbell—or at least, what I assumed was the doorbell—went off.

I'd been in the middle of the book, and the detective in question had just figured out that he was being stalked by the very man he thought was killing girls in his small town. It wasn't a sophisticated thriller, but it was definitely intense, and I'd been about to start frantically checking the final pages of the book for the detective's name to figure out whether he survived the coming encounter when the chimes thundered through the house.

When I came back down to the chair and put my heart back where it belonged, I scowled in the direction of the elevator.

How exactly were you supposed to answer the door when the door was an elevator? Would it just open up when whoever it was asked for it to? Was there some sort of peephole that would tell me who was in there?

I went over all the ways Roger couldn't possibly know where I was again and confirmed that there was zero opportunity for him to have figured it out. First of all, Roger wasn't exactly a rocket scientist. He wasn't even a mediocre detective. Second, no one in their right mind back at home could have foreseen me somehow hooking up with a guy rich enough to live in the penthouse of what I was guessing was the nicest building in Minneapolis.

Hell, no one had even known I was coming to Minneapolis. I hadn't even told Alice.

So there was zero way for Roger to know I was here.

And with that thought, I got up and strolled toward the elevator, wondering how the hell I was going to pull this off and whether I should use the card Leo had left to call his office and find out whether there was a standard operating procedure for someone showing up unannounced at his... door.

"Hello?" I called when I got to the elevator, feeling ten shades of stupid. "Who's there?"

"Delivery from Blackard's, Ms. Olivia," a voice called back.

I jerked backward at that. A delivery? From Blackard's? I knew the place. Everyone knew the place. It was the fanciest store in Minneapolis—and all of Minnesota, for that matter. The place you went if you wanted to blow literally thousands of dollars on clothes.

What were they doing with a delivery here? And why did the guy know my name?

"I didn't order anything from Blackard's, I'm afraid," I called back.

I couldn't even afford a purse from that place, much less a whole delivery.

"Mr. Folley did," the woman answered. "He ordered quite a bit, actually. He requested that we deliver it here and take back anything that you don't want."

I stared at the door, so confused that I couldn't come up with an answer for at least a full minute.

"Who the hell is Mr. Folley?" I finally asked.

And why the hell was he sending me a delivery from Blackard's?

Even more importantly, how did he know I was here? And did he have any connection to Roger?

I YANKED THE PHONE away from my ear and stared at it for a second, so shocked at what he'd said that I thought he had to be joking.

"Are you joking right now?" I asked, slamming the thing back to my ear. "You ordered everything the store had and just had it... sent over?"

"Well, I assumed that you'd want to have a look at everything they had," Leo replied, his voice a whole lot calmer than mine was. "And I also assumed that you'd want to try things on before you decided. I don't really see what the problem is here, Olivia."

"The problem," I replied sharply, "is that some lady just got off the elevator with about fifty garment bags full of stuff."

"Am I wrong, or were clothes one of your terms? Clothes and hot water, I believe you said."

I could hear the smile in his voice.

I sort of hated that I was already smiling back at him, even though he couldn't see me.

I didn't want to think this was funny. I didn't want to think this was anything other than a convenient way to get a roof over my head and some safety for a couple of days. I definitely didn't want to be laughing and shaking my head at this guy, who was either smoother than anyone I'd ever met before, or quite literally the most naïve person ever when it came to women.

"Is this your thing?" I asked. "You get a woman in your house and throw all the clothes she can handle at her until she gives in to whatever you want?"

He snorted. "This is definitely not my thing. I don't generally throw clothes at a woman to try to get her to give in to whatever I want. Honestly, I've never bought a woman clothes in my entire life. That's why I had them send the whole store. I wouldn't know where to start."

I echoed his snort.

Like I said. Either incredibly smooth or incredibly naïve. I had no idea which one it was.

And I really hated that I was sort of falling for it. Because this was only about the next week. I was only here for a week, and then I was gone. Once I got the money he promised me and I was able to pay for a hotel, I was out of here. Plain and simple.

No arguments.

And that meant I didn't have the time or the freedom to get attached to him. Like, at all.

I straightened my face, tipped my chin up, and made my heart as hard as I could manage. *Up, walls. Down, emotions.*

"So you're saying that because you're too lazy to pick out clothes, I have to do it for you."

"Hey, you said you wanted clothes so you could perform. If you've changed your mind, I can just have them all sent back—"

"No!" I said, far too quickly.

Hey, I was getting really tired of the two outfits I'd managed to bring with me. And he was right. Clothes *had* been on my list of requirements. "I'll work something out," I said grudgingly.

"I'm sure you will. Just send whatever you don't want back with Linda. She'll take care of the bill," he replied.

The line went dead. But not before I heard him chuckling at the predicament he'd just handed me.

The bastard.

CHAPTER 8

OLIVIA

"RIGHT," I TOLD THE Linda in question, setting the phone carefully back down in its cradle and wondering what the hell he was doing with a home phone in the first place. Weren't landlines essentially a thing of the past at this point? Along with fax machines and record players?

Or did rich people still keep them?

Either way, it wasn't my problem.

Right now, my problem was the woman still standing in the elevator, surrounded by garment bags.

"Linda? I guess you'd better come in. Here, let me help you with that stuff. I'm sure your salary doesn't also cover weightlifting in the name of random millionaires who decide to buy the whole store."

She snorted and rolled her eyes at me. "You would be awfully surprised. When you work at a store like Blackard's, you end up doing a whole lot of stuff you never thought you'd do."

Intrigued, I grabbed as many garment bags as I could carry—while praying that I didn't wrinkle everything inside by layering said bags so heavily—and asked what she meant.

It turned out Linda had a degree from the very same university I myself had attended. Only she'd been studying the marketing side of business, while I'd been studying the numbers and accounting side of things. Before I knew it, we were not only lugging bag after bag out of the elevator—which I'd figured out how to pause so that it stayed where it was rather than running off with thousands of dollars' worth of clothes—while comparing notes on the school, the campus itself, and professors we'd shared.

"The diner on the corner right before campus starts," I told her when she asked me where my favorite place had been. "I went there for everything. Study sessions. A way to escape my roommate my freshman year. Coffee in the middle of the night. All the pickles I could eat."

"Oh my goodness, the pickle bar!" she giggled. "I'd forgotten about that! Though that might be a repressed memory. I made myself sick one night eating too many pickles, and I haven't been able to really enjoy them ever since."

I laughed, surprised and more than somewhat pleased to find someone so... well, close to my own level in a place like this. I mean, I'm not going to lie; I'd been feeling out of my league pretty much since the moment I'd stepped into Leo's place. The entire penthouse bled money, and it had taken me 0.2 seconds to realize that he could have whatever he wanted, whenever he wanted it. Hell, he'd probably grown up that way, given how naturally he moved around in the sheer luxury of the apartment.

It was a far cry from the world I'd grown up in. Single mother who was always attracted to the wrong sorts of people. One-bedroom apartment without enough furniture for the two of us, since the best she'd been able to do as far as working was full-time waitress in the local restaurant. Jeans that were too short because I outgrew them before we had money to buy new ones. Shoes that were too small, for the same reason.

A dad who, according to the rumors, had all the money in the world but had never wanted to spend any of it on the kid he'd never acknowledged.

Yeah. Like I said, my mom had a history of hooking up with some real winners. Roger definitely hadn't been the first.

I jerked my attention back to Linda and what she was saying, telling myself that this was not the time to go down the rabbit hole where my father lived, and realized that she'd just asked me a question.

"I missed it," I said. "I'm sorry. I was too busy wondering what, exactly, all these bags could possibly hold."

"The entire store, in three different sizes," she said, her voice turning practical. "He thought you'd wear a 4, but my experience with men is that they have absolutely no idea about these things. So I also grabbed everything in 2 and 6. That way you don't get stuck in a dress that's too small and pants that are too long."

"You might actually be my new best friend," I told her honestly. "So how do we do this?"

She grinned, the girl who had made herself sick on pickles suddenly appearing again. "You try on. I sit and watch and give opinions. And then I collect a big, fat commission check."

I grinned back, leaned in, and whispered, "Then let's make sure I buy one of everything."

Which was exactly how I ended up doing what amounted to a fashion show for my new friend Linda, who not only had a business marketing degree from one of the best universities in the country, but also, it turned out, had an amazing eye for fashion and fit. When the first dress I tried on didn't fit exactly right, she pulled out a magic cushion full of safety pins and started nipping and tucking until the dress fit me like a glove.

"Magic," I said simply, staring at myself in the mirror. "You're a witch. That's the only possible answer."

Her grinning face appeared at my shoulder in the reflection. "I am, but keep it down. Just imagine how the guy who runs the store would react to that sort of thing."

We moved on from there, to slacks and blouses and hats and shoes and then to cocktail dresses and stuff that was even more formal than that, me moving through the outfits slowly and taking my time to enjoy the feel of the expensive material against my skin, the way the dresses fell in heavy, well-tailored folds.

The fact that expensive shoes somehow seemed to fit better than the cheap kind I usually had to buy.

When we got to the more formal dresses, though, I frowned and looked up at her, confused. "I understand all the rest of this stuff," I said. "For dates and the like. But where on earth am I going to wear *these*?"

She just shrugged. "Mr. Folley said you'd need a formal dress for the charity auction. I didn't know which you'd like best, so I brought them all."

Ah. The infamous charity auction. The deadline to our little race.

Right, well, formal dress it was, then. I couldn't exactly refuse to go to the event for which he'd hired me in the first place.

"Got anything in blue?" I asked. "It's the best color for my eyes."

Linda tipped her head, stared at me for a moment, and then nodded and started rifling through the remaining garment bags, evidently knowing already which one she thought was going to be best.

. . ⁂ . .

TWO HOURS LATER, LINDA was gone—leaving her card and her personal number behind so we could get lunch at some point—and I was in my room, staring at the bags she'd left behind.

I thought we'd done a pretty fair job of buying at least half of what she'd brought along with her. So I'd followed through on my promise to get her a big commission.

But what was I supposed to do *now*?

A bath, I realized, the very idea sending a thrill of utmost pleasure through my body and bringing goose bumps along with it. I wanted a bath.

Yes, I'd already had one this morning. Or at least a shower, which was like a bath that took more effort. Yes, I had a bath last night.

And yes, I damn well wanted another one right now.

After all, plenty of hot water had been one of the stipulations of my agreement. I wanted to make sure I was getting my money's worth.

But I wasn't going to do it in my bathroom. I'd seen Leo's bathtub on the quick tour of the apartment last night, and I knew his tub was roughly twice the size of mine. Not that mine was small. Plenty of room to stretch out and luxuriate, especially for a short girl like me.

But twice the tub meant twice the hot water, twice the bubbles, and twice the bath salts. And there was no downside to that.

Besides, he wasn't home, and a quick glance at my watch told me that he probably wouldn't be home for two hours or so. Getting off work at five was pretty standard in the corporate world, and he struck me as the kind of guy who probably worked more rather than less.

I had plenty of time to borrow his tub, get through a relatively lengthy bath, and get back out of the water and into clothing again before he got here.

Also, they'd put locks on doors for a reason, and one of them was to keep the guy you were sort of accidentally living with out of the bathroom where you were taking a bath.

Right? Right.

I nodded to myself and marched to the kitchen, where I started rifling through the cupboards, looking for wineglasses. If he liked old books and leather this much, I was guessing there was good wine to be had as well, and nothing went better with a bath than good wine. I found the glasses I was looking for in a cupboard that I could reach without even having to get on the counter and found an entire shelf of wine in the walk-in pantry.

I grabbed a bottle of red that was probably way too expensive to be handled so roughly, found a corkscrew in the silverware drawer, sent a thankful thought toward the office where Leo was probably currently doing something really boring and wine-less, and then made for the master suite and the enormous bathtub held within it.

I LAY BACK AGAINST the side of the bathtub, set my wineglass back down on the side—which had, thanks so much, plenty of room for wineglasses and the books I'd brought with me—and swung the table-type thing over the water.

This. Was. Heavenly. I'd definitely been right about the larger bathtub being better, because it had not only come with more space for hot water, but also better toys. The larger sides were one thing. They gave me more room for setting stuff down. But this swinging table thing, complete with a depression for a wineglass and a prop for a book?

Heavenly. Probably the best thing any man had ever invented. In fact, I was betting a man hadn't invented it. It was the sort of thing only a woman would think of.

I moved my wineglass over to the little table, then dried my hands on the towel I'd brought with me and grabbed one of the books.

The water was hot, the bubbles were popping, and the bath salts were fizzing away under the surface. Even better now that I was submerged in hot water for the third time, I was actually starting to feel clean. And I didn't have a care in the world right then.

"Just me, my book, and a bottle of wine," I sang softly, jigging a little bit with the tune.

This wasn't where I'd seen myself a week ago, but I had zero complaints.

"Olivia?" a voice suddenly called out, booming through the open door and into the cavernous bathtub.

I jerked, sure that I was hearing things. *Praying* that I was hearing things.

"Olivia?" the voice called, sounding louder now.

More insistent.

Oh shit.

When I heard my name, my first thought had been that Roger—or one of the goons I imagined he had—had managed to find me and somehow get up the elevator and into the apartment. But now that I'd heard the voice again, I realized that I was wrong. That wasn't Roger, and it wasn't one of his goons.

It couldn't be. Unless Leo himself was somehow one of Roger's goons.

Because I recognized the voice that was calling my name. That was Leo.

He had evidently decided to come home early instead of working all the way to five like a normal human being would.

I exploded up out of the tub, my instincts acting before my brain could manage anything, and the table in front of me went flying upward as well—along with the wineglass and the book. I was up and climbing over the lip of the tub when both of those things—which I hadn't really thought about until that second—came crashing down.

The wineglass hit the floor with a horrible, incredibly loud shattering sound, and a moment later, I heard the *splat* of the book hitting the bubbles in the tub.

I didn't have time to turn around and try to save it, though, as I was slipping and sliding through wine and glass fragments on my way to the door that I'd left open.

Because my brain had finally kicked in, and it was telling me one thing: get to the door and get it closed before Leo got here. It was bad enough that he was going to figure out that I was in his bathroom taking a very bubbly bath in his tub.

He didn't need to actually *see* me doing it.

I'd told him I wasn't a prostitute, and that was the truth. I didn't need to expose my bare flesh to him. No matter how attractive I found him.

I went skidding across the floor, my wet feet hitting a patch of evidently very slippery wine, and then, quite suddenly, I was starting to lose balance. My feet were sliding faster than they should have been—possibly thanks to the bubble bath I'd added too much of—and I felt myself starting to tip. Overbalance. Head toward the floor.

I had a split second to think about how badly this was going to hurt, and then I was flying right into the cabinet he had against the wall. My feet and legs hit it first, and the thing actually splintered under the pressure, sending all the knickknacks on top of it flying to the ground in a clattering racket that sounded like it could have drowned out screaming. If I'd even tried to scream.

I hadn't. I wasn't a screamer.

Not that it mattered. I didn't think I could have made more noise if I'd actually been trying.

I went to the ground with another *splat* and grunted, groaning as bare skin hit hard tile flooring.

Shit, this wasn't good. None of this was good.

"Olivia?"

Crap, he was coming down the hall! And I didn't have time to get to the door. I knew that now. Particularly with my newfound inability to get anyplace without sending myself to the ground.

I turned around, scrambling, and made for the bath. Bubbles. Water. That table thing.

I hadn't wanted him to find me in there, but at least if he did, I'd be hidden.

I was halfway there when I heard him opening the door.

"Olivia, are you—"

I hurdled the side of the tub like a freaking Olympian and splashed down in the water, then turned to look at him.

Shit, how much had he seen?

And double shit, how much trouble was I in?

"I'm sorry," I started. "I wanted a bath, and I thought I'd see what it was like to have one in such a large tub, and then I got out because you were here, and I broke your wineglass and—"

PERFECT STRANGER

He put a hand up to stop the babble, his mouth pulled tight as he tried to suppress the smile that was trying very hard to erupt on his face. "You're fine," he assured me. "I don't mind at all. Use the tub anytime you want. I did, after all, promise you as much hot water as you could stand."

His eyes dipped down to the bubbles below my chin and then flew back up to my face, his own face a bit more flushed.

"Um, are you good in here? Have everything you need?"

I wanted to go under the water and drown myself, if that was what he meant by having everything I needed.

I didn't think it was.

"I'm good," I said. "But I ruined one of your books."

"I'll survive," he said solemnly. "As long as it wasn't the Poe."

"It wasn't," I assured him. "I've never really understood him, to start with."

He looked shocked at that. "You've never understood Poe? Blasphemy!" Then he turned serious again. "But that flaw in your character aside, do you want dinner? I came home because I was starving. Shish kebobs for dinner? Do you like peppers? I like peppers. Maybe too much."

Now he was babbling almost as much as I was.

This whole situation was a freaking nightmare.

"Shish kebobs sound fine," I told him.

To my surprise, he nodded and then turned and left without saying anything else.

I stared at the place where he'd been, wondering what the hell that had been about. Then I got out of the tub, fished the book out as well, and started to get dried off. Now that he'd mentioned it, I was starving, and shish kebobs sounded amazing.

I just hoped he was a better cook than he was a liar.

Not that I could blame him. If I had a stranger living in my house, I would go out of my way to get home early as well. Though I'd tell them that I was doing it and skip all the subterfuge.

CHAPTER 9

LEO

I WENT TO BED AFTER a dinner filled with laughter and talking, feeling full and more than a little bit drunk off wine and good conversation.

If this was what it was like to have someone living under the same roof as me, it wasn't half-bad. In fact, it wasn't even half-bad. It wasn't bad at all.

It felt a whole lot like something I'd been waiting for most of my life to find. And that didn't only go for my adult life, either. I'd been a lonely kid, growing up in an enormous house in the suburbs with brothers who had a nanny watching after them, while my parents worked like their very souls depended on it. Sure, I'd gotten to see them on weekends.

Sometimes.

But that wasn't the same as having them around all the time, and it hadn't taken the place of having siblings that were closer to my own age, either. I'd had some friends at school—not many of them, but still—and I'd seen how their families were. Full of kids and laughter and weekend outings. Moms lecturing about homework and dads trying to teach their sons to love baseball.

Family units like mine had never been.

In a way, I guessed, the loneliness was in my upbringing. Maybe even sunk down into my soul. And I'd always thought that it would be that way for the rest of my life. After all, what does a guy who doesn't know how to have a relationship with another human being know about... well, having a relationship with another human being?

How was a guy who didn't know how to have a girlfriend supposed to get one? Much less get someone to live with him?

Evidently, I thought with a smile, he found a girl living in her car in the alley next to his office building and offered her a trade. A roof over her head in exchange for her agreeing to play arm candy for a week.

Maybe more.

Because at the end of the day, that was really all Olivia was: a hired gun. Arm candy for the week. A shield that I could use against Meghan so that she wouldn't lecture me about the press—for a week at least.

I hadn't expected it to turn into a sudden urge in the middle of the day to go home and see what she was doing. I definitely hadn't thought it would be me hanging on her every word as we sat at my never-before-used dining room table (I usually ate in front of the TV or standing up in the kitchen), eating pasta and drinking as much wine as we could hold.

Not that she'd been saying anything I could use to actually figure out that much more about her. Nothing about her past or her family, and still nothing about how she'd come to be living in her car. She didn't even give me a good reason for having taken me up on my deal.

Something that I was definitely still wondering about. It had been a very odd and definitely spur-of-the-moment suggestion from me, this wild scheme for her to live at my house and pretend to be more to me than the girl I found living in her car. And I'd definitely had second thoughts—like this morning when I left for work and realized that I was leaving a total stranger in my house on her own.

But had she? Had she thought that it might be dangerous for her to be here, in my house, without anyone else to turn to if things got dicey? Had it even occurred to her that it might put her in a bad situation?

If it had, why had she agreed to it?

They were questions that she wouldn't answer when I asked them, which seemed, at this point, to be par for course as far as Olivia Cadwell went.

At least I'd learned her last name over dinner. That, I supposed, was a start.

It also seemed woefully inadequate to know nothing more about her than her name when she was literally turning my life on its side with her presence. Rearranging my books. Bogarting my tub when I was at work. Filling the penthouse with the scent of the bodywash she'd ordered from the market and put on my account.

Making so much noise in the bathroom that I'd run in there, horrified that she'd be dead on the floor when I arrived, only to see her very pert, extremely toned ass as she scooted back into the tub.

And that wasn't all I'd seen. She'd turned and slid into the water, but not before I'd had an eyeful of equally perky breasts, her rosy areolas and nipples hard at having been out of the water.

I took an involuntarily sudden breath at the memory of that bare flesh glistening with water as it slid down into the bubbles, her mouth caught in an O of surprise at having been discovered, and my fingers started tapping against the bed in a rapid, needy staccato.

It had taken every ounce of willpower I'd had in that moment not to go to her, jerk her out of the tub, and tell her I wanted her right then and there. And the only reason I hadn't done it was remembering that she was a guest in my house.

Not some girl I was allowed to take advantage of.

She wasn't a girl I'd brought home from a date, having been set up by one of my friends. She definitely wasn't a girl who was only here because I was an eligible bachelor or one of the richest guys in the city. She wasn't looking for anything from me.

Except hot water, food, and a roof over her head for the next week.

I'd forced my face into something that I hoped was casual—maybe even amused—and asked her if she was all right. And I'd done everything I could to keep my eyes on her face rather than letting them dart down to where I could still see the swell of her breasts over the water.

Damn, the woman was sexy. And smart as hell, with a quick tongue and a sarcastic sense of humor.

If I'd been set up with her by one of my friends, I would have spent the entire first date trying to get a second one. But she wasn't here for that.

And I had to keep that front and center in my mind if I was going to get through that week without making a colossal fool of myself over the brightest woman that had ever been in my house.

• • ❧ • •

I WOKE UP ON A GASP, my body arched up off the bed and coated in sweat, my hand on my rock-hard cock, already stroking.

I jerked and pulled my hand away, trying to figure out what the hell I was doing... and why.

And then I remembered. It all came rushing back into my head like a fucking avalanche. If an avalanche was made of white-hot lust and glowing blue eyes.

I'd been dreaming. Dreaming about Olivia in the tub. Or rather... dreaming that she hadn't gotten back into the tub at all.

Instead, I'd run into the bathroom and found her on the floor, her body stretched out and wet with water, steaming on the floor like some sort of illusion. She'd gotten up, intent on getting back into the tub, but instead of allowing her to go, I'd moved toward her and taken her in my arms. She'd moved up against me, the wet heat of her soaking through my clothes until I was almost as wet as she was, and she'd looked up at me with those eyes and apologized in something that was a lot more sex and invitation than real apology.

So I'd done the only thing it was possible to do in a dream where I was very obviously caught in a bathroom with a girl who was wet and naked and ready for me.

I'd turned her around so her back was to me and bent her over the lip of the tub—which had suddenly been right in front of us, since dreams have a very flexible idea of spatial awareness. I'd leaned down and run my lips over her ear, asking if she was sure she wanted me.

She'd arched her back and pushed her ass against me, and that had been all the answer I needed.

I had to say, Dream Leo had been a whole lot more sure of himself than Real Life Leo had ever been. Dream Leo hadn't even questioned it. I'd stood back up, spread her legs, and run my fingers slowly up between them, biting my lip as she gasped and bucked for me when my fingers found her center. I'd put one hand on her hip and slid the fingers of the other into her, holding her still while I explored her, moving my fingers in and out, rotating them to hit the spot I somehow knew she wanted me to hit until she'd come for me, a groan of sheer pleasure ripped out of her throat.

And then I'd stood her up, wrapped my hand in her hair, and begun to tease her with my cock. Because I was suddenly naked instead of clothed, thanks to that weird dream thing.

Before long, I'd been sliding into her, my eyes closing in sheer bliss at how hot and tight she was. I'd bent her over again, for better access, and slid deeper, harder, faster—

I gasped as I came out of the memory, my hand working up and down on my cock now at the echo of that feeling. The imprint of her body on my mind as she rode me in reverse, her hips rocking and bucking against me, begging me to come for her. Begging me for more as her mouth told me we shouldn't be doing it. We shouldn't be doing any of it because she was nothing more than a guest in my house.

My hand sped up, moving up and down with increased urgency as I got closer and closer to coming, my mind still in the hot, steaming flesh of Olivia's back as I fucked her, her wild hair bouncing underneath me, her head thrown back in sheer ecstasy...

And then I was coming, both in my memory and in real life, the heat spurting out of me as I bit my lip to contain the groan that wanted to fly out of my mouth, my fist tight around my cock and my back arched up off the bed in pleasure.

And I was coming for her, her body fresh in my mind, her laughter in my ears, her name on my tongue, and it was the most intense thing I thought I'd ever felt.

And when it was over and I was lying back, my breath ragged and my heart galloping away, I realized it was going to be a whole lot harder than I had realized to have her living under my roof... and sleeping in a bed that I didn't have access to.

Which was most certainly a problem I hadn't considered when I'd first asked her to come stay at my house and pretend to be my girlfriend. Just for the week. Just until the charity auction.

Lying here now, still thinking about how her body might feel under me, I was starting to wonder whether "just a guest" and "just for a week" was going to be enough.

Because I wanted more. Even with how little I knew about her and her constant reminders that she was only here for the week, I wanted more.

The problem was, I had no idea whether "more" was even remotely an option with Olivia Cadwell.

CHAPTER 10

LEO

I GAVE HER THE CELL phone I'd bought her over breakfast. She was right in the middle of a plate full of strawberries—another thing she'd ordered when she decided to call down to the market—and instead of taking the thing I was holding out, as I'd expected, she simply stared at it for a long, tense moment.

Then she looked up at me, her face carefully expressionless.

"What the hell is that?"

"It's a cell phone. Surely you have them where you come from."

Look, I knew from her slightly different accent that she'd come from a different part of the state than I had, and I'd also started to figure out from the way she talked that she didn't come from a large city. She was from a small town.

That was the extent of my guessing on the matter, and she hadn't given me anything else to go on.

But I was willing to bet that no matter how small the town might be, they'd still heard of cell phones. There were a lot of places in Minnesota that didn't get good coverage and probably didn't have an electronics store on every corner like we did here in Minneapolis, but surely they still knew what the devices were.

She was also smart enough to have been outside of whatever small town that was. Way too sharp to be truly sheltered.

I lifted my eyebrows as I waited for her to respond, though, starting to question whether there were actually places where these things weren't the norm.

Her eyes slid down to the phone and then back up to me again, and I saw that she knew exactly what it was... and didn't want anything to do with it.

"We do," she said. "I threw my own out the window on my way here. Why do you think I need another one?"

I didn't answer for a moment, my mind too busy trying to interpret what she'd just said. Cut it up into little pieces and examine them one by one, trying to figure out exactly what that meant.

Why would she have thrown it out the window? When she was on her way here? Why had she been on her way here? Alone? Without money or credit cards?

And evidently without a phone?

The mystery around this girl was deepening, and I was starting to really wonder what she was hiding in all of those shadows.

Then again, this wasn't the time to sit around thinking about it. I needed to get her to take this phone—or at least consider taking it—so that I could get to work.

"I want you to have a way to get in touch with me if you need me," I said simply. "And a cell phone is the easiest way to make that happen. It also gives me a way to get in touch with you. You know, if I happen to want to talk to you. I'm not saying it'll happen, but it might. And if it does, a communication device might come in handy."

Her mouth relaxed a bit at the levity of my statement, but she didn't smile.

She also didn't reach for the phone.

"If I need you," she said, "I'll find a pay phone."

I almost laughed, except that she was dead serious about that statement. "Are there pay phones still? I don't know when I last saw one."

"There are," she replied, straight-faced. "I was coming out of one when I ran right into you."

And now I did chuckle. "I guess I was too busy being run over to pay attention to where exactly you'd come from."

"Understandable," she allowed. "But that doesn't change the fact that there are pay phones out there, and I'm quite capable of using them."

"A cell phone would be a whole lot easier, though, don't you think? More portable. Easier to get to. Doesn't take change. Or give you a time limit."

Another slight relaxing of the mouth. But still no agreement.

And I was running out of time. I had a meeting this morning that I couldn't be late for, and if she wasn't going to give me a real reason for not taking the phone, then I wasn't going to play this game. At least not right now.

Later, I'd ask her again why she was being so weird about taking the phone.

Right now, I just needed her to take it.

"Look," I said. "I don't need to know why you don't want it, though I'm going to ask again later. But as long as you're staying under my roof and pretending to be my arm candy, I'd like you to carry it. Think of it as part of your disguise. And as a form of protection. If you need me, I want you to be able to get a hold of me immediately. I want to be able to get to you before..."

She frowned. "Before what?"

The thing was, I didn't know. I'd been about to say, "before anything bad happens," but now that I was actually thinking through that, it sounded insane. What was I, some kind of hero, rushing in to save the day when she was about to get in major trouble?

No.

But that didn't change the fact that I wanted to be that hero if she needed one.

"In case you need a knight in shining armor," I told her, keeping my voice light so she'd know I was joking. "I want to be right on the other end of the line if you need anything. Is that so much to ask? I've put the phone on my plan, and it's in my name, so you don't need to worry about how many minutes you use or anything like that. And it'll make me feel better."

And at that, her mouth relaxed all the way, and she finally smiled and took the thing.

It didn't give me any answers for why she was so scared of it. But her having it was a start. And it was really the most I could ask for right now.

"My number is 612-708-5342," I told her. "Program it in so you can get in touch with me quickly if you need to."

She made a face at me. "I don't need it in the phone. I've already memorized it."

"You've what?" I asked, shocked.

"Memorized it. You know, learned it by heart? Surely even you know what that means." She gave me a quick, playful grin and then repeated my number back to me.

So first she didn't want the phone, and now she didn't want to store my number in it.

What the hell was this girl hiding?

Or, if I looked at it another way, what the hell was she running from?

"Fair enough," I told her with a smile. "But don't blame me if you forget it right when you need to call me and ask me to bring something important home. Or are in the midst of being kidnapped."

She rolled her eyes. "If I'm being kidnapped, I doubt they're going to let me keep the phone in the first place," she said. "But no one would try it, anyhow. Superhero, remember?"

I laughed and then, much to my own surprise, leaned forward and gave her a soft kiss on the cheek.

Equally surprising was the fact that she didn't pull away from me. Instead, she seemed to actually lean into it.

The thought built a fire deep inside me, and I felt my skin go hot at the memory of what I'd dreamed last night... and what I'd done afterward. This girl was not only a mystery, but one that was managing to work her way right under my skin.

Something no one had ever done before.

"I'll see you when I get home," I said. "Do you want me to send more clothes today?"

"Hell, no," she groaned. "I'm having lunch with the woman who brought them, though. We're going to discuss the merits of a business marketing degree versus an accounting degree."

I tipped my head, confused at what that had to do with anything, but then glanced at my watch and realized I was officially late. I took one more sip of coffee, grabbed my briefcase, and headed for the elevator, leaving the girl who was almost certainly running from something—or someone—safely behind in my kitchen, finishing her own coffee and what I thought had to be her third bagel of the morning.

I wondered what she'd be doing when I got home and then grinned to myself at the thrill that ran through me at the idea of coming home to her at all.

. . ∽ . .

"WHAT'S ON THE SCHEDULE for today?" I asked Janice as I walked into my office after the meeting.

She reached out, grabbed her notepad, and hustled after me, already reading through my schedule for the day. "The first and most important thing is to start doing interviews to replace Jonathan," she said in her most no-nonsense tone of voice. "The sooner you can get someone in here, the better. Especially if Jon is going to train them."

"He gave me an indefinite amount of time to find someone," I reminded her.

"And he lied to you," she responded. "I know his wife, and I know she's not going to wait forever. I'd give it a month, tops. After that, you're going to be out of luck."

I sighed heavily. Leave it to Janice to know more about the situation than I did. I seemed to be surrounded by women who had more information and were better prepared than I.

Not that I was complaining. But it would be nice to get the drop on one of them at least once.

"In that case, I suppose I need you to start setting up interviews for me," I told her. "Let me guess. You've already been through the resumes and have several likely victims picked out."

She gave me a tiny grin of acknowledgement. "I sure do. I don't know what you'd do without me, honestly."

"Neither do I," I told her, well aware that it was the truth. "Put them into my schedule and let me know when they're coming up. Send me the resumes you're choosing so I can get acquainted with the applicants. Anything else?"

"A check for the charity auction."

"Already done," I replied, more than a little bit proud of myself. I wasn't planning on buying anything this year, so I'd done a straight donation, and it had been twice as big as it was last year.

Folley, Inc. had had a very good year. I liked that it gave me the leeway to give more money to the city's leading charity—particularly because their goal this year was to raise enough for a new school in one of the lower-income areas.

Janice frowned at me, though, like I'd done something wrong.

"What?" I asked, surprised.

"Did you run this by Meghan?"

"No. The last time I checked, she wasn't the one who controlled the money in this company."

"She does control your reputation, though." She jerked out her phone and started typing quickly. "I don't suppose you put your name on that check or asked for any credit to be given to you?"

I sighed. "No. If you ask me, it defeats the purpose of giving money if you ask for credit. I didn't do it so people would think I was cool."

She leveled a cold stare at me. "You should have done it just to keep Meghan off your back. Don't worry. I'll handle her."

She turned and left without another word, which, I guessed, meant the rest of my day was free.

And right now, I knew exactly what I wanted to do.

I reached out, grabbed my phone, and dialed the number I'd programmed into it.

"Leo, I'm not in trouble. I have not been kidnapped, I am not in the middle of a robbery, and I do not currently need assistance. I could, however, use some more bagels, if you wanted to pick them up on your way home."

The words were cold, but there was a smile hidden behind them, and I grinned.

"How did you know it was me? Did you finally program my number into your phone?"

She snorted. "No, but the number came up when you called, and I have it memorized. Why is that so hard to believe?"

It was hard to believe because no one ever memorized phone numbers anymore. Particularly after they'd only heard them once.

"I just don't often meet people who can memorize numbers so quickly," I said. "I'm not sure how to handle it."

"Did you call just to ask me how I memorized your number?"

"No," I said honestly. "I called because I wanted to hear your voice."

She paused for a moment, like that had surprised her so much that she was—for once—at a loss for words. Then, her voice gentler now, she said, "Well, you've heard it. Do you feel better?"

I did.

And I wasn't entirely sure I liked that.

After all, I only had this girl for a week. I'd promised myself that I wasn't going to get used to having her there, and I wasn't going to let my guard down.

And yet here I was, calling her in the middle of the day just to hear her voice and getting all warm and fuzzy about it.

This did not bode well for my ability to keep myself sheltered from the situation.

CHAPTER 11

OLIVIA

I STARED AT THE CELL phone in my hand, my mind churning and my stomach doing something that felt even worse than churning.

Honestly, for such a little thing, the phone itself was making me feel like the entire world might actually have turned directly onto its side. It was a potato bag trying to shake me out of it. A shoe coming down to squash me. A laser in the sky, making me its target.

Okay, okay, I hear you. I was being incredibly dramatic, and I wasn't even coming up with very good metaphors.

But seriously, a laser in the sky that's trying to target you? Can you imagine what a great movie that would make? In fact... Isn't there a video game that's got exactly that plot?

Still, back to the cell phone.

I slid the thing across the table just to get it away from me and watched it come to rest against the jug of iced tea I'd taken from the fridge earlier.

It sat there, like some sort of ticking time bomb. And I stared at it. You know, the way you so often stare at bombs when they're sitting on your kitchen table, just waiting to explode.

Okay, right, I know. The drama.

It wasn't actually a bomb. And it wasn't going to explode. So far, the only thing it had done was take a call from Leo—the guy who was letting me stay in his house and eat his food, and who had actually bought me the cell phone in question. And the truth was, I could understand why he'd done it. He was letting me stay in his house, for shit's sake, and leaving me here on my own—something that I still didn't entirely get. Sure, he said he needed a cover for some of the public appearances he needed to make, and I'd essentially been in the right place at the right time to land the gig.

But he was incredibly rich. He owned a freaking company, to start with, and who knew how much real estate. He was wildly good-looking, and we're talking could-model-the-best-brands good-looking. Tousled brown hair that looked like he'd just gotten out of bed looking like the $1,000 that haircut probably cost. Piercing blue eyes that could also turn hazy and gray under the right conditions. Broad cheekbones, sharp jaw.

Freaking chin dimple.

That chin dimple alone should have been able to get him whatever girl he wanted in the entire city. The money wouldn't have hurt, either. I hadn't exactly been around him much yet, but I was betting he wasn't exactly hurting for dates. No, there weren't any pictures of women in his house—there weren't any personal pictures at all, actually—but that didn't mean they didn't exist.

And even if they didn't, I was sure he could have gotten them.

Hell, if he needed a girl, I was even more sure I'd heard about high-end escort services that provided that sort of thing.

So why in this great state of Minnesota had he chosen me, a girl who had been living in her car outside of his office and who had almost hit him once when she was trying to get her favorite parking spot?

And why had he then brought me to his house, bought me clothes, fed me and bathed me and told me to make myself at home? Why had he left me here alone, when I could be anyone, ready to get up to all sorts of shenanigans?

None of it made any sense. The phone, though, did make sense, and I thought it probably had a lot to do with the idea that as long as he was going to leave me alone in his house, he wanted a way to be able to track me while I did it.

The tracking, though... that was the problem. Not tracking from Leo, who I was starting to think might just be one of those Good Guys you always heard about. No, I wasn't that concerned about him being able to get in touch with me whenever he wanted to.

The truth was, I kind of liked the idea of him being able to call me. I liked the idea that I could call him, too.

Though I wasn't going to admit either of those things to anyone else.

The problem was, though, that *anyone* might be able to track me. The moment anyone else had that number, if they were intent enough on finding me, they might be able to use the tech in the phone to do it.

Shit.

I was getting so paranoid that I could hardly stand myself.

I reached out, grabbed the phone, and dialed the number of the one person who had always been able to talk me down from the ledge. Because right now, I needed her.

"Alice?" I asked when she answered the phone. "I need you."

"What happened?" she asked, her voice immediately serious. "I'm coming. Where are you? How can I find you? Are you safe? Are you missing a leg?"

I took a moment to feel all sorts of relieved at the familiarity of her overreaction and then snorted. "If I was missing a leg, Al, don't you think I'd be doing something a little more dramatic than just telling you I needed you? Like... I don't know, screaming?"

"Maybe you're in shock," she said quickly.

Now I laughed outright. This right here was exactly why I needed Alice. I was sitting by myself freaking out about the possibility of Roger using some probably not-yet-invented tech to grab the signal from my cell phone from his family room and track me down, and she was worried that I might have had my leg cut off in—

"How exactly do you think I might have lost my leg in the first place?" I asked, trying to force the words around the grin on my face. "And why exactly do you think you'd be the person I would call for that?"

I could hear her judgment of me when she spoke again. "I don't know, Olivia. I'm your best friend. I guess it comes with some responsibilities. Like saving you when you've had your leg cut off. Which I take it you have not. So what do you need help with?"

Right. Down to business. "My legs are both still intact, so it's not that," I replied. "It's... everything else."

And I told her everything. I described the penthouse and told her about the suite I had at my disposal. I told her about Leo himself and how insanely nice he was being—and how I didn't trust it. I did not tell her about how he'd seen me falling all over myself trying to get back in the tub before he could see me.

I figured I was allowed to keep some things to myself.

I did tell her, though, about the cell phone and how terrified I was of using it.

"Olivia, you're being paranoid," she said bluntly. "I don't think anyone but the cops can trace phones like that."

"You've met the guy," I said, my tone just as blunt. "Do you blame me?"

A pause followed, and I could practically see her screwing up her face, the way she always did when she agreed with me but didn't want to tell me so because she was afraid that agreeing with me would encourage my bad behaviors.

Yes, Alice had always been like a fifty-year-old woman caught in a younger body. It was one of the things I found eternally amusing about her.

"I don't blame you," she finally said. "In fact, I think you're right. There's something going on with that guy, Liv. Something weird. He showed up here yesterday looking for you. Not your mom. He specifically asked for *you*."

My heart dropped down into my stomach. "And what did you say?" I asked quietly.

No one knew where I was, specifically, but Alice had the best idea. And Roger must have realized she would.

That had to be why he'd gone after her. He'd known I wouldn't tell my mother anything because she'd tell Roger. So he'd gone after the one person I thought I could trust.

"What do you think I told him?" she asked, all sarcasm. "I told him to fuck right off and never come to my house again."

I fizzed with laughter. "That's my girl," I said. "I've got to go. Leo is supposed to be home soon, and I don't want him to find me on the phone when I made such a big deal of taking it in the first place. But Alice?"

"Yeah?"

I bit my lip. This girl was like a sister to me. She was the most important person in my life. I hated that she was still in the same town as Roger, hated that he might still have access to her.

I hated that I didn't know what the hell he was doing or why—or what he might be capable of.

I couldn't protect my mother. I knew that, at this point. But I could sure as hell try to protect my best friend.

"I don't trust him," I told her firmly. "I don't know who he is or what he's doing, but he's intent on finding me, and I'm afraid he'll do whatever he needs to do to get that done. You be careful, okay? Don't go out alone at night, and make sure your doors are always locked. And maybe stop driving your car."

"What, you think someone might put a bomb in it?" she asked, trying—and failing—to hide the smile.

I scowled. "It's not unheard of."

"I don't think Roger is smart enough to know how to wire a bomb," she said. "But I'll be careful. You, too. After all, you're the one he's after."

I hung up with that thought weighing heavily in my mind... and then went to have another bath.

After turning off the phone.

I was in a place he didn't know, staying with a man Roger had never even heard of. He couldn't find me here. As long as I was careful.

As long as I didn't do anything to draw attention to myself.

CHAPTER 12

LEO

I LEFT THE OFFICE EARLY.

Again.

And it wasn't only because the day had been dragging on for hours and I was already heartily sick of having to go through the resumes Janice was continually sending for the opening in the accounting department.

I mean... Well, it was partially because of the sheer number of resumes I was having to look at. There were millions of them—or maybe just ten to twenty—but they were all so obviously bad fits for the position. I'd looked at line after line of experience from people who just didn't seem like they'd fit with the environment I'd built—or who would handle the insane amount of pressure we went through every single day—and by the end of two hours, I thought I might start screaming soon.

Shocking to think those were the resumes that had been held up above the others and actually passed on to me for consideration.

So yeah, that two hours of looking at job applicants was part of the reason for my early escape.

The other part was currently holed up in my penthouse, doing heavens knew what with the new cell phone I'd given her and the entire apartment to herself.

As I rode the elevator to my floor, though, I caught myself grinning at my own reflection in the wall. Because I was betting I did know what she was doing.

I was betting it had a whole lot to do with the bathtub in my bathroom, a book, and another bottle of my favorite wine.

When the doors opened into the apartment, the first thing I heard was music blaring from someplace within, though, and I immediately canceled the thought of the book. Evidently, she was having a dance party rather than a book club meeting.

Though I supposed the wine was still a distinct possibility.

Grinning, I walked through the hallways that led past the library and the living room, wondering what, exactly, she was doing that required such loud music. The place looked like it was intact, and there was no one else here, so it wasn't like she was having a party or anything like that. A quick glance at the kitchen as I passed it told me she wasn't cooking, and another glance into her own bedroom—the door was wide open—told me that she wasn't in there.

I paused and tipped my head, my eyes on the hallway past her suite of rooms.

The only thing left on this particular hallway was *my* room, and that seemed odd. But this was definitely where the music was coming from.

Then I realized that my room held something that she'd already shown keen interest in.

The tub.

I shook my head and started forward again, wondering exactly how many baths she planned to take... and whether she was using the same scent she'd been using before.

The one that had stuck in my room until I'd gone to bed that night and kept visions of her in my head into my dreams.

When I got to the door of my room, I inhaled deeply, and realized that yes, she was using the same scent again. Something that smelled like vanilla but wasn't quite. It was muskier than that. Deeper.

Not as sweet.

In short, it was everything that Olivia herself was: sweet, but not underneath. Underneath, there was something a whole lot darker that I couldn't quite name.

Something that I didn't think she didn't want to let me see. Something she was keeping hidden about herself.

Three steps forward and I was at the door of the bathroom, my ear tipped down to listen. The door itself was open, and the room was filled with steam, which made me think several things: 1. She hadn't taken a bath, she'd taken a shower, and 2. She must be finished, as I could no longer hear the shower running.

In fact, I didn't hear anything in there except the music.

Maybe she wasn't in there at all anymore.

The thought brought with it a sort of sinking, disappointed feeling, though I pushed that away from me the moment I recognized it. I had no right to be disappointed that this random girl—who I barely even knew—wasn't in my bathroom having a bath the way she had been before.

No. In fact, I should be relieved to find her gone rather than in here so that I could use my own bathroom. Have my own shower. Sit in here and do whatever I wanted.

And now I just sounded petulant and childish, for no good reason.

I didn't want a shower. I didn't want to sit in here and read a book or whatever else I might do. I wanted to find Olivia here and ask her how her day was. Tell her what I'd done with my own day and why I was home early again. Tell her what I thought we might do tonight.

Which was, of course, even more insane. Because like I said, I hardly knew the girl. Why the hell would I be so intent on finding her in my bathroom and talking her ear off about...what? What had I even said?

I was clearly losing my mind. It was really the only possibility. And I was also talking to myself. Neither of these things seemed like a good sign.

I pushed the door open and walked through the steam, having convinced myself that she wasn't actually in here but had for some reason left the music on after she was finished with her shower.

Which made it a whole lot more surprising when I got to the bathtub and found myself looking down on a floating—and entirely naked—Olivia in my bathtub.

. . ❦ . .

FIVE MINUTES LATER, I was in the kitchen drinking wine like my life depended on it. The wine was to give my hands something to do and steady my nerves. Unfortunately, it was doing absolutely nothing to quiet my brain, which was humming with the memory of Olivia stretched out in the tub, all stark white skin and dark hair, the strands floating out around her head like she was some sort of sea nymph or something.

The woman was unbelievably beautiful. I'd known it from the first time I'd seen her, but seeing her lying in the tub, her eyes closed and her face completely relaxed, I'd realized it in a way I'd never thought of it before.

And no, it wasn't only because she was naked and so perfect that I hadn't been able to stop myself from staring at her. It was a whole lot more than that. I mean, yeah, her body was incredibly beautiful, her breasts pert and perfect, her waist incredibly tiny, her legs longer than I would have imagined possible.

But that wasn't what made her so beautiful.

It was the relaxation, I realized. Without the constant movement and defensiveness, her face was...

Otherworldly. It was a stupid, dramatic word, but it was the only one I could think of to describe her.

And I'd had it right before I'd realized that I was staring at the girl naked in my tub. I'd jerked and opened my mouth to apologize, my thoughts already trying to cram themselves out of my mouth to make up for the fact that I was there. And then I'd realized something else.

She was asleep.

She was floating in my tub, asleep, while rock music played in the background with so much volume that I'd somehow gotten into the bathroom and all the way to the tub without waking her.

And thank goodness for that. I didn't know Olivia well yet, but I knew her well enough to think that she very definitely wouldn't be happy with the idea of me walking right in on her in the bathtub.

I'd crept back out, the sight of her branded on my eyes, and made my way to the kitchen. To drink wine, try to get my brain to stop spinning around her beautiful face, and wait for her to not only wake up, but realize that I was in the house and come looking for me.

And in the meantime, I'd learn to pray to the universe or whatever other benevolent being was listening and thank them that she hadn't been awake.

When she appeared, she was wrapped in my bathrobe and still steaming from the water. I knew she was coming because the music suddenly cut off and her footsteps sounded down the hardwood of the floor.

I took another gulp of wine and then put the glass down on the counter, wondering if I was really going to be able to pull this off.

It just wasn't every day that I had to pretend I hadn't seen a girl naked in my tub.

Olivia got to the kitchen, turned her eyes to my glass of wine, and then looked at me with one lifted brow. "Home early from the office and day drinking? It must have been some day."

And just like that, I remembered why I'd come home early. I wanted to talk to her. Wanted to tell her what had gone on during the day and get her opinion on what I could do about any of it. I wanted to hear her thoughts about the world and the people in it and complain about my publicist and what I was being forced to do.

I had known Olivia for about two days, and I already felt as if she might be one of the only people in the world who truly listened to me.

I pushed the bottle toward her wordlessly and turned to get another glass from the cupboard.

She watched me with both eyebrows raised now and then said the best thing she could possibly have said. "Shall I order? Italian?"

"Hell, yes," I moaned. "I'll have spaghetti with meat sauce. Call the place on the corner. They have my card on file."

She smirked a bit at this hint that I ordered from said restaurant far too often, then grabbed the cell phone that she'd left lying on the table and started searching for the place's information.

. . . . . .

WE'D GONE THROUGH TWO bottles of wine and all the food—plus all the bread—by the time I remembered that I'd been planning to ask her out for dinner.

"I thought we could go out," I said, sliding my plate away from myself.

Olivia tightened the belt on my bathrobe—which she still hadn't taken off—and grinned. "I'm pretty sure we did. Only we stayed in to do it. And I didn't have to get dressed up."

"Which is a crying shame," I said, raising my glass and realizing as I said the words that I was probably more than a little bit drunk. "You look great when you get dressed up."

She frowned. "How would you know that? You've never seen me dressed up."

I tipped my head, wondering how I'd known it as well, and then realized that it was better to have said that than to tell her that I knew what she looked like completely undressed.

The moment the thought was in my head, though, it was the only thing I wanted to say. As so often happens when you're drunk and trying desperately not to say a specific thing.

"I am assuming," I told her very carefully. "Say," I continued, thinking it would be better to stop talking about her clothes—or lack thereof—entirely. "I have a question."

She leaned forward and made her eyes big. "You do?" she whispered, definitely making fun of me.

I narrowed my own eyes at her, stuck my fingers into my wineglass, and flicked wine at her, not caring that it would also get all over my own bathrobe. "My family is having a party this weekend," I told her firmly. "I'd like for you to come meet my brothers and my parents."

The joking expression left her face immediately, and she sat back, suddenly extremely serious. "Meet your family?" she asked, sounding like this was the last thing she'd expected—and the most terrifying thing in the world.

"Why do you sound like this is the equivalent of being burned at the stake?" I asked, confused. "They don't bite. I promise. And I think they'll really like you."

She bit her lip. "And what if I say no?"

I reached out and tapped her once on the nose, grinning. "You can't. You made a deal, remember? All this hot water you're using? The flip side was that you'd play arm candy."

"And you actually *want* them to meet me?" she asked quietly.

Now it was my turn to pause for several long moments.

What, exactly, was she asking here? Why was she acting like she wasn't good enough to be allowed to go out in public?

I leaned on my elbows and bent forward over the table so I could get closer to her. "Olivia," I whispered. "You are one of the most fascinating people I've ever met in my entire life. You're smarter than most of the people who lead my company, and you're insanely beautiful. I would be proud to introduce you to them."

A slight frown creased her brow, and then she leaned forward as well, mimicking my pose. "Really?" she murmured.

My eyes went right to her lips. Those lush, perfect lips that had moaned my name as I'd taken her from behind in my dream. The lips that had smiled up at me when I touched her.

I flushed at the memory, my cock going suddenly so hard I could barely sit still, and then I noticed that the bathrobe had come open, exposing the curve of one breast.

I yanked my eyes back up to Olivia's and found hers dark and glassy with a sudden need.

Damn, she wanted me to kiss her. And I wasn't sure I'd ever wanted anything more in my life. My fingers twitched with the need to reach out to her, my blood heating to the point of pain, and I started to move toward her.

Then she jerked and looked down, realizing she was coming undone, and pulled back.

"In that case, I'd love to go," she said in a voice that was far too loud and far too casual.

Her eyes flicked to mine, full of the knowledge of what had almost happened.

But she didn't lean toward me again. Instead, she stood up. "I'd better get to bed. This much wine always makes me sleepy. I'll see you in the morning, Leo."

She pranced away before I could say anything else, leaving me sitting at the kitchen table with a throbbing cock and pounding heart, and the knowledge that we could never, ever drink wine together again.

Not unless we were going to the same bed afterward.

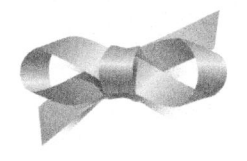

CHAPTER 13

OLIVIA

THE NEXT MORNING CAME far too early, and it was only partially because of how much wine I'd had to drink at dinner.

Mostly it was because I'd been awake for hours after I got back to my room, thinking about what had happened—or almost happened—between Leo and me. Thinking about that smoldering look on his face when he leaned in, all smoke and wine and hot, hot sex.

I'd thought I was going to melt on the spot, and it hadn't only been the wine talking. I'd known the man was handsome, but damn, he'd managed to amplify that in the space of about three seconds with that slow, sexy lean and the things he'd started saying to me.

Look, I knew I was smart. I'd gotten amazing grades in high school and had gone to one of the best universities in the nation. I'd been on track to become valedictorian, too, before I had to move home to get my mom out of some trouble.

I'd been on my way to a star-studded career full of business and numbers... before it had all come crashing down.

But I also had a dad who'd gotten my mom pregnant and had then run as fast as he could and had refused to have anything to do with me ever since—despite the fact that he knew exactly where we were and how to get in touch with us. He'd communicated with my mom often enough to make sure she didn't dare tell anyone who he was, and more often than not, I'd found her crying on the floor of her closet after they spoke.

I had a general idea of who he was and how much money and power he had. And I had a very firm understanding that he didn't want one damn thing to do with us... and never, ever sent money to help.

And you'd be surprised how much something like that crawls right into your soul and sticks. You'd be amazed at how you go through your entire life never really feeling like you actually belong, or like anyone actually wants you—even when you know for a fact that you're being ridiculous.

And with all that in mind, you'd be even more amazed at how someone feeding you compliments, even when they don't know the first thing about you because you've been refusing to answer any of their personal questions, goes right to your heart and digs its nails into you.

I was already melting at the look in his eyes, which had told me quite clearly that he wanted to kiss me.

His compliments had made it impossible to breathe.

And the burning ache between my legs had made the whole thing even worse.

In short, I'd been in way over my head and more than three sheets to the wind. I was about to close my eyes and dive right in, lips-first, when I realized what I was doing.

I didn't know this man. I didn't know what he wanted or why he was complimenting me or even why he'd picked me up off the street and taken me home. I didn't have one damn clue what he might actually be after. And as long as I didn't know that, then I couldn't trust him.

I definitely wasn't going to let myself fall head over heels for him. Which was exactly what my heart had been trying to do at that kitchen table after my fair share of two bottles of wine.

So I'd gotten up, made some quick excuse, and come to my room. Where I'd promptly locked the door and shoved a table in front of it.

Just in case he decided he might want to test my resolve with a midnight visit.

If he had, I wasn't sure I would have had the self-discipline to turn him away. So it was better for everyone involved if I'd made sure he couldn't get into the room in the first place.

Also, please see what I said above about not knowing if I could trust the guy. I was on the run from one guy who might or might not want to kill me. I didn't need to make myself vulnerable to another guy with questionable motives.

Yes, I knew how it sounded and that I was being dramatic. Yes, I knew Leo hadn't ever done anything to make me question his motives.

But I also knew that I was only going to be here for another week or so, until this infamous event, and then I was going to be back out on my ass again and living in my car, unless I came up with a plan. I didn't want to make that living in my car with a heart that I'd broken by leaving the guy who had been supporting me behind.

Walls up, Olivia, I told myself firmly. *Emotions down. And keep it that way.*

I couldn't afford to fall in love. This was just a short-term gig, and short-term gigs didn't leave room for emotions.

So I'd run to my room, locked the door, and spent the rest of the night aching for a man I knew I couldn't have... and telling myself it was better that way.

This morning, I was definitely looking... well, not well rested. I didn't look *bad*, I thought, leaning forward and staring at my reflection in the mirror. Nothing that a little extra makeup couldn't cover. Darker circles under my eyes than I liked, and a shadow behind my eyes that came from knowing I had to make a decision I didn't want to make.

Good thing I wasn't seeing anyone I knew today. My friends and family would have spotted the signs of stress immediately.

I was just going to have to hope that Leo's family didn't look as closely as Alice and my mom would have.

"NERVOUS?" LEO ASKED, his hands firmly on the steering wheel of his roadster.

I forced a laugh. "What do I have to be nervous about? I meet parents and brothers of the guys I'm accidentally living with all the time."

I saw his grip tighten on the steering wheel. "So you accidentally live with guys all the time? How does meeting their families usually go?"

Was he... jealous? I glanced at him out of the corner of my eye and saw that he was trying very, very hard to make this whole thing a joke.

The creases at the corners of his mouth said he was lying.

"Oh, you know," I said breezily—because I liked the guy, and if I could do something to lighten the tension, I was going to do it. "I act my ass off and charm the pants off of everyone around me. Just your normal Saturday in Olivia's world."

He smiled then—a real smile—and shot me a quick glance. "Do you go out of your way to charm the pants off everyone you meet, or is it just a natural side effect of your personality?"

"Natural," I said with a shrug. "It's been happening all my life. At a certain point, you get used to it and start to use it when you can. Now, what do I need to know about this family of yours? I assume we're supposed to look like we've known each other longer than five minutes."

"Longer than five minutes would be good," he agreed. "Let's shoot for six months. Though we've only been dating for two."

"Six months, dating for two," I muttered. "Got it. Now give me the low down on your family."

He grinned, accepting this partner-in-crime scenario, and started talking.

BY THE TIME WE GOT out of the city and to the country house where his parents had retired, my brain was so full of Folley Family Information that I was starting to wish I'd brought a notebook along with me for writing stuff down. I'd never needed that sort of thing before, but I was generally trying to remember numbers, which didn't have as many complex relationships as it turned out Leo's family did.

"So you're the oldest, named after your dad. Next is Ben, who's ten years younger than you, and then Nick, who's eleven years younger than you. Jeez, no wonder you felt lonely when you were a kid. They were a duo, huh?"

"They sure were. Always getting into trouble together. Always a team. And I was just the boring older brother."

I reached out and poked him in the ribs. "I bet you weren't that boring. I bet you got all the girls and were head of the debate team."

He rolled his eyes. "By the time I was in high school, I was already learning how to run my dad's company. I didn't have time for the debate team. Or girls. I was lucky I got to college at all."

He was still joking, but I could hear the pain behind the words. His dad had gotten cancer when Leo was only fourteen, and though there had been CEOs and CFOs and all those other initials to run the company, Leo had been fast-forwarded as heir apparent and had started learning the company early. His dad had recovered but hadn't been able to go back to work, so Leo had been running the place since he graduated from college.

No small feat for a twenty-one-year-old.

"So basically you've been supporting the family since you were a kid," I interpreted. "No wonder those shoulders are so broad and muscular."

He turned to me, his eyes going dark, and I bit my lip, knowing it would only take a couple of words to push this situation over into the territory we'd accidentally discovered last night.

Knowing that I could shift my own position just a little bit and give him the invitation he was so clearly waiting for.

My body screamed for me to do just that. I could already feel my back starting to arch, my hips starting to rock for him.

My brain, though, was shouting even louder and telling me that I couldn't do anything of the sort. We were sitting in his mom and dad's driveway, to start with, and though I didn't really care that much what they thought of me as I was going to be gone next week, I didn't think Leo would be too pleased if they came out and found us making out in his car.

He would, after all, have to speak to them again.

So I drew back and gave him a sassy grin. "Brother Ben and Brother Nick are still in grad school and college and are both earning business degrees. I'm sure they'll start helping you carry the load soon. Right?"

I watched him pull himself back as well, his eyes getting lighter and his chest seeming to contract. Shit, it was like he was actually getting smaller, and a part of me felt really, really bad about what had to look like some sort of dismissal from me.

It wasn't. But it was the safest thing for both of us. I didn't know who was after me or what they might do, and I didn't plan to stick around in any one place for long to find out. Even if that place belonged to Leo Folley, Billionaire Playboy with Plenty of Money and Security.

I didn't want to bring trouble into his world. And a niggling little voice in the back of my head told me that if Roger found out where I was, that was exactly what would end up happening.

"One can only hope," he said seriously. Then he grinned. "You ready?"

"Ready as I'll ever be, I suppose," I said, grinning back. "You?"

"Olivia, I was born ready," he said in a growl.

I didn't even have to ask him what he meant by that. I could tell from the look on his face. But I turned away from him, knowing for a fact that I couldn't take him up on that.

Not now, and not ever.

But damn, did I want to.

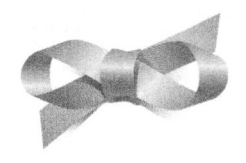

CHAPTER 14

LEO

BY THE TIME WE GOT home from dinner with my family, Olivia and I were both so exhausted that we could hardly make it to the elevator without falling down.

Say what you will, but driving two hours to get to their house, having a full dinner with wine included, and then driving two hours back is exhausting work. Especially when this particular dinner included my parents—and brothers—asking Olivia every question they could think of and eventually deciding that they liked her so much that we should stay for coffee and dessert and a family movie night.

Actually, "liked" isn't a strong enough word. They had freaking *loved* her. There had been one tense moment when they asked her how we had met, and she'd floundered before I stepped in to tell them that she'd almost hit me with her car and I'd forced her to go to lunch with me as a penalty, but aside from that…

She'd been brilliant. Beyond brilliant. She'd been everything I could have hoped for.

So much so that my mother had actually pulled me aside in the kitchen and told me that she hoped I'd manage to make this one last.

Which had, of course, broken my heart into tiny, tiny shards. Because "this one" wasn't going to last at all. Olivia was just a girl doing me the favor of playing my arm candy for a week to get Meghan the publicist off my back about my reputation. She was here to make some appearances with me and get her picture taken rather a lot and say all the right things to the press about how wonderful I was and how she hoped it would last forever.

She wasn't here to stick, and though I'd gone out of my way not to think about that, it was the truth.

The other truth was that at the end of the day, the dinner party with my family had been a bit of a test run. I hadn't really wanted her to meet them, because I knew how much my parents wanted me to settle down, and I hated to get their hopes up with a girl. At the same time, I'd needed to know if Olivia was going to be able to handle the pressure the press would put on her.

If she could handle my mother, she could handle the press. And I thought that meant we were probably going to be just fine.

I stumbled out of the elevator, Olivia's arm in mine and her steps heavy, and put the rest of those thoughts behind me.

I was too tired tonight to think about what would come after the charity auction.

After Olivia walked out of my life again.

For tonight, I wanted another glass of wine, a shower, and my bed, and I didn't plan to let anything get between me and those things. As for Olivia, she was already looking toward her room.

"I've had enough of the world and my thoughts for the day, Leo. I'm going to sleep."

"You and me both," I told her. "I want a shower, and then I want oblivion. Thank you for coming with me today. It means... a lot."

She gave me a dreamy, fuzzy sort of smile, full of fatigue, and then, to my complete surprise, stood on her tiptoes and pressed her lips to my cheek. "I like your family," she said softly. "Almost as much as I like you. It was my pleasure."

She turned and headed toward her room before I could respond—and, I thought, before she could think too hard about the fact that she'd just kissed me and acted like it was completely normal to do so.

• • ❦ • •

THE NEXT MORNING, OF course, that dreamy, hazy mood of hers was gone, and she was all business again.

"What are you doing today?" she asked over coffee, her eyes on the paper in front of her.

"I promised Jack I'd help him move some furniture at his house, so I'm heading there. Why? What are *you* doing today?"

She didn't answer my question. Just like she never answered my questions. "Who's Jack?"

"Best friend."

"What are you moving around?"

I laughed. "Knowing Jack, it's something incredibly practical like a grand piano. But I really don't know. I didn't ask when I said I'd take the job."

She slipped a strawberry into her mouth and watched me as she chewed. "Aren't guys like you supposed to have people who do that sort of thing for them? Like... moving guys, at the very least?"

"You'd think so, wouldn't you?" I asked. "But Jack likes to leave things until the last minute, and that means the treasured moving guys aren't available. I am, I fear, a sad replacement."

"Oh, but you've got big, broad shoulders and strong arms," she said, grinning. "I'm sure you'll do just fine."

"That's so kind of you," I said wryly. "Do you want to come help?"

"No," she said immediately. "I've got some stuff I have to do."

Well, there was my chance again.

"What are you doing?"

She stood up abruptly, leaving her bowl of strawberries only half-eaten. "Stuff." Then, before I could ask again, she leaned down and pressed a kiss to my forehead. "Have fun moving the pianos. Be careful of your toes."

I stared at her as she walked out, wondering whether this kissing thing was going to be a new trend, what it might mean, and why the hell she refused to answer questions every time I asked them.

The girl was, at this point, a walking mystery, and it was starting to get frustrating. I'd known her only a few days, granted, but she was literally living in my house and sleeping under my roof, and yet she refused to open up to me. I didn't know her story or how she'd come to be sleeping in her car, and though I would have sworn that there was something in her past, something she was running from, I couldn't get a handle on what it was.

Mostly because she wouldn't give me any information.

The thing I did know was that she'd run into trouble at some point. It was the only answer for her being so nervy about the phone. I didn't know if she'd given me her real name, and I still didn't know where she'd come from.

Worst of all, I didn't know how the hell I was supposed to help her if she wouldn't let me in.

Not that I was interested in playing white knight, you understand. It was just that she was currently under my protection, and I couldn't do a very good job of taking care of her if I didn't know what she needed.

Seriously.

I SHOVED AT THE PIANO until it was in the spot Jack had chosen for it, grumbling to myself about best friends and how much they liked to take advantage of certain people's time and energy.

"Tell me again why you even have a piano?" I grunted, shoving one last time and then standing back and taking it all in. "Do you even play?"

"You know as well as I do that I don't," he said primly.

"Right, that's what I thought. So... tell me again why you have a piano?"

He gave me a very wicked, very sly grin. "Because the girls who come over here don't know that I don't play piano. And they like it when I say that I do."

I shook my head at him, full of disappointment, but didn't bother to say anything.

I knew from very long experience that it didn't matter what I said. Jack was still going to be Jack, regardless of what the more responsible adults in the room thought of it.

Jack, seeming to know exactly what I was thinking, changed to a very sly, very nosy grin. "But enough about me. Tell me, how is your lady friend doing?"

I blew out a slow breath, allowing myself to think before I answered him. I loved Jack. I really did. He was my oldest and best friend, and if I had problems, he was the person I went to, without fail.

But I still only told him about half of what I thought. Because over and above anything else, Jack was a gossip. He couldn't keep a secret to save his life, even when he knew he *should* keep it. And there were certain things I didn't want being made public about my relationship with Olivia.

Namely, the way I was starting to feel about her.

It was already going to be a circus out there when the press got a hold of the fact that I was dating someone. They were going to be all over both of us with questions, and most of those questions were going to be incredibly personal and inevitably inappropriate.

They would be even worse if they knew how much I was starting to like the girl.

Which is why I only said, "She's driving me crazy with her unwillingness to answer questions about herself, if you want to know the truth."

Jack leaned up against the piano and did his best impression of Frank Sinatra. "She won't tell you the truth?"

I shrugged. "I don't know if she will or not. She won't answer any of my questions to start with. I have a girl living under my roof that I don't know a thing about, and every time I start trying to get to know her, she puts up more walls than I would have thought possible. It's like trying to see through a freaking brick wall."

He narrowed his eyes at me like he was trying to see through *me*. "And why, exactly, do you need to know anything more about her than the name she's given you? She's only staying through the charity auction, right?"

As if I could forget. "Right."

"And that's next week. Right?"

"Yep."

He shrugged nonchalantly. "Then why does it matter what her life story is? After that auction, you're not going to see her again. It won't matter who she is or what she's done. It only matters that she gets you through the night and helps you improve your rep so Meghan lays off. At least... I thought that was the plan." His gaze grew even narrower. "Unless something's changed."

And that right there was the spot where I was going to stop answering *his* questions. Because things had changed.

And it was precisely none of his business why.

"I'd just feel better if I knew more about her, that's all," I said vaguely. "I mean, she's living in my house. Would you want a girl living in your house that you didn't know anything about?"

He leered. "If she looked like Olivia, I wouldn't give one single damn about her past."

I snorted. "That I can believe."

He got serious again at my tone. "If it bothers you so much, hire a PI. Have someone else do the research. People might want to hide their background. That doesn't mean it's always possible."

I turned away without answering. I would never hire a PI to learn more about her. Everything about it felt wrong. Intrusive. Petty.

And even if I did, and he found out everything she'd ever done, from the one time she got a parking ticket to where she'd gone to school, it wouldn't change the fact that I wanted *her* to tell me, and she wouldn't.

No, I didn't know why it mattered.

And yes, I'd been wondering that for the last four days. Because it shouldn't have.

I should have been able to blow it off as easily as Jack was. The fact that I couldn't do it was driving me almost as crazy as Olivia's unwillingness to answer questions.

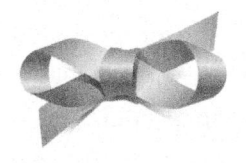

CHAPTER 15

OLIVIA

BREAKFAST THE NEXT morning was... testy.

And by "testy," I mean we were both eating in the same space, and that was about the extent of it. We were having breakfast at the same time, and we were eating roughly the same thing—granola with strawberries. The latter was because that was what Leo had pulled out for breakfast, and I didn't want the strawberries to go bad.

The former was just bad luck.

Because believe me, if I'd known he was having breakfast when I slid out of my room with coffee and something solid on my mind, I would have turned around and gone right back in. It would have been a whole lot easier for me if he'd already left for the office by the time I decided that I needed to eat.

Instead, I'd somehow managed to arrive in the kitchen at the exact same moment as him, and that meant that unless I wanted to take one look at him and turn around and leave, I was going to have to actually sit down and eat in the same space as him.

And before you ask, there were several reasons for the general awkwardness. The first was that he'd come home last night full of questions and had been peppering me with them all through dinner. It was annoying and frustrating and tiring because I knew for a fact that I didn't plan to answer any of them and had told him so time and time again—to no avail.

When he asked me why I didn't want to talk about it, I'd just sealed my mouth and refused to say anything else. I didn't think he was ready for the real answer, which was that I might like him, but I didn't trust him, and the lack of trust meant that I wasn't going to tell him one damn thing about who I actually was or where I'd come from. I also didn't think he was ready for the other real answer, which was that I was afraid to tell him.

I didn't want him to get it into his head that he needed to actually protect me from Roger, and from what I knew about Leo, that was exactly what he'd do. Shit, he'd probably call Roger up directly and tell him that this little grudge, or whatever it was, was pointless and that Roger would be better off going away and living his life without thinking any more about me.

And while that was sweet and everything, he didn't know Roger. He hadn't seen the mean glint in the guy's eyes when he went after my mother. He hadn't seen the triumph flashing across his face when he knocked her to the floor and then told her that she needed to stop being so clumsy.

He definitely hadn't heard the fury in his voice when he told me exactly what he'd do to me if he caught me saying something he didn't like ever again.

No, that wasn't the sort of guy who would just take *You're better off letting go of this grudge* lightly. The truth was, I thought he was probably the sort of guy who would hear something like that and immediately decide he'd have more fun attacking the person who had said it. And then doing something to their entire family as well.

Okay, sure, I might have been overreacting. But that didn't change the bone-deep fear that came up anytime I thought of him. And I wasn't going to lead Leo toward him intentionally. I just wasn't going to put Leo in that sort of danger. Period.

So I wasn't answering questions.

I popped a strawberry into my mouth and chewed it, congratulating myself on that solid, bulletproof logic.

Then I allowed myself to think about the other reason that we were being awkward with each other this morning, and I almost choked on my congratulatory strawberry.

Because the other reason didn't have anything to do with me trying to protect Leo, unless you were going for me trying to protect him by keeping him out of a messy romantic entanglement with yours truly.

We hadn't talked about it last night, but that scene on the drive home from his family's house was still clear and present, right smack-dab in the middle of my mind. Him turning to me with dark eyes and parted lips. The way my body had wanted to go all gooey and sexy on me. The feel of my blood suddenly running a whole lot hotter than it was supposed to.

That combined with the scene from the night before, when we'd had far too much wine and gotten far too close to each other over the table, had brought a whole new awareness to my mind, and I was thinking I probably wasn't the only one there. I'd seen the way he stiffened when I got too close last night, when we were cooking dinner. I'd heard the hitch in his voice when he told me goodnight once we got home from his family's house.

I'd felt myself standing on tiptoe to kiss him on the cheek without thinking twice about it.

We had suddenly gotten way too comfortable with each other, and the physicality of it was inviting a whole lot more than just Girl Stays in Guy's House to Do Him a Favor.

This was a whole lot more like Girl Stays in Guy's House with a Side of Sexual Tension.

And man, was that side wreaking havoc on my body. It had taken me what felt like hours to go to sleep last night just because I'd been thinking about the way he looked when he caught his bottom lip between his teeth whenever he was thinking about something.

I'd been thinking about him using those teeth for a whole range of other things.

And thinking about stuff like that right before bed is not exactly good for falling immediately asleep, let me tell you.

I glanced up at the man in question, swallowing the strawberry, and saw that he was also studiously avoiding my eyes, his reading glasses on and the paper in front of him. He looked like he could well have been eating breakfast alone for all the attention he was paying to me.

Maybe he preferred to be alone for breakfast. Maybe I was cramping his style. Maybe he couldn't wait to get to this charity auction thing so I would get the hell out of his space.

I couldn't say why, but thinking that made me feel a whole lot better. Like it was a life raft in the middle of a storm or something. So I grabbed it and held on tight, telling myself again and again that I just needed to get through that auction, get the money he had promised me, and then get the hell out of here.

Get the money, get out of here, get a hotel, I chanted in my head. *Get the money, get out of here, get a hotel.*

Easy peasy.

Walls up. Emotions down.

And speaking of being alone. I had some plans for the day, but they weren't going to happen if Leo hung around for too long.

"Aren't you going to be late for work?" I asked, not even trying for charm.

He snorted, no doubt noticing that I didn't exactly sound like I wanted to crawl into his lap and make nice. "Actually, I'm working from home today," he said.

I was actually surprised at that. "You can do that?"

He looked over his glasses at me. "I own the company, Olivia. It's not exactly easy for me to stay home, but if I decide I want to, I don't exactly have a boss telling me that I can't."

Okay, that was a fair point. I just didn't think CEOs did things like taking days off. "Are you doing something important here or something?" I asked, doing my best to soften my voice and sound like I was just making conversation.

He shrugged. "I don't like going out in the rain."

And at that, I finally felt myself starting to soften a little bit. "Do you melt if you get wet or something?"

He leveled another very serious gaze at me. "I do. Why do you think you haven't actually seen me taking a bath or shower?"

Damn, he was good at that. His mouth didn't even twitch or anything.

I leaned in, though, dropping my voice as well. "Probably because I don't walk into bathrooms where people are very obviously taking baths. Or showers," I said, matching my tone to his.

And then he finally cracked a smile. "Right, you've got me there. I don't melt in the rain, but days like this always make me want to stay home and be lazy. I can't really—I'm not that lucky—but I can fool myself into thinking I'm taking a day off by working from here rather than going into the office. I guess you could call that a fair trade."

I tipped my head at him, seeing the guy in an entirely different light with just that one small admission. "You don't like going out in the rain?"

"Or the snow," he admitted. "It always feels like it was a day off from school, so it should also be a day off from work. I don't know—call it wishful thinking, I guess."

"Or call it what it is: you're the boss, and no one can tell you you're not allowed to."

Another impish grin from him, complete with flashing eyes. I noticed they were sky blue today, which I took to mean he was happy. Or at least relaxed.

"I am the boss, and no one can tell me I'm not allowed to. I called in sick this morning, too, so my assistant will be doubly impressed when it turns out I did some work after all."

"And they don't catch on to the fact that you call in whenever it rains or snows?" I asked doubtfully. "Are they actually that gullible?"

"Jealous, probably," he said with a shrug. "I'm of the pretty firm opinion that everyone in the world would call in sick when the weather is bad if they could."

I lifted my coffee mug in a faux salute, deciding that that opinion was enough to make me want to call a truce with him. At least for today, when we were evidently going to be stuck under the same roof. After all, I couldn't stay mad at him just because he had questions and was insanely, unfairly hot.

Right?

"To staying home for a rainy day," I toasted.

He picked up his own mug and tapped it to mine, nodding. "To rainy days. Unfortunately, I can't take the entire day off."

I took a sip of coffee, frowning at the idea of taking a rain day but not being able to actually take the day off. "No? Important business?"

"Extremely. Numbers stuff. I hate doing it, but it's important for that whole running-the-company thing."

I felt my interest rise by several notches. It had been ages since I'd had anything that felt like it was stretching my brain out. "Numbers? Want me to have a look?"

He cringed. "I would do it in a heartbeat, but it's private company information. I couldn't let you see it unless you'd signed the standard company NDA."

I actually snorted at that. "What do you think I am, some sort of corporate spy or something? Who managed to con you into letting me into your house by staying in my car for long enough in the alley outside of your building? Come on. What do you think I'm going to do with that information? Use it to start my own identical company?"

He gave me a long, serious look and then nodded. "Well, seeing as how I'm the head of the company..." He reached down and slid the stack of papers I hadn't even noticed toward me. "Have at it. My job today is to figure out why the bottom line isn't matching up to what it should be and then figure out how to fix it. And I'd sooner shoot myself in the foot."

I cocked an eyebrow at him—math wasn't *that* bad—and then looked down at the papers. A quick scan showed me that this was a range of accounts for the company that showed the spending of the employees in a certain department. "Employees who have expense accounts?" I asked.

"Yep. And the totals we're getting from the head of the department don't match what he told us to expect for the quarter. I have to go through all of that and figure out why."

I scanned the columns, the numbers lining up quickly in my head, and before long, I saw the hole.

"You're missing numbers from someone," I said, sliding the paperwork back toward him. "This can't possibly be an accounting of everyone in the department. Not with the total he gave you. Or else he's lifting money off the top, though I can't imagine anyone would be stupid enough to make it so obvious they were doing that."

He stared at me for a moment, then looked down at the papers... and then looked up at me again. "How did you do that?"

I just shrugged. It wasn't worth going through my process and trying to explain it. "I told you, I'm good with numbers."

At that moment, my cell phone rang, and I glanced down to see a number I recognized as Alice's. "Gotta take this," I said. "Have a good rain day."

I got up, grabbed my phone, and walked out of the room, already wondering why Alice was calling me on this number when I'd specifically told her not to.

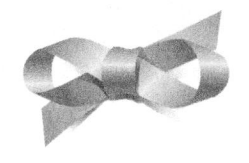

CHAPTER 16

LEO

I STARED AT JANICE, trying very, very hard to keep myself from groaning. Or screaming. Or punching a hole in the wall.

Because none of those things would be helpful, I told myself firmly. They would, in fact, be the opposite of helpful. Right now, I was keeping it together. It might be close, and I might be riding a razor's edge of 'together,' but I was still handling things.

Barely.

Giving in to the screaming going on in my head would most definitely mean I stopped keeping it together.

"Well, that didn't go well," I said, forcing my voice to be as steady as possible.

Janice widened her eyes and pressed her lips together like she was also trying to keep from screaming, and considered me for a long, tense moment.

Then she grinned, her dimples popping out and her eyes snapping at me.

"Didn't go well?" she asked quietly, forcing the smile down a bit. "Is that what you call the guy basically having a panic attack in the middle of the meeting? Because I was thinking a whole lot more along the lines of a total shit show."

I grinned back at her, unable to stop myself. "That was my first thought, but I was sort of afraid to say it. Sounds unprofessional. Aren't CEOs supposed to... I don't know, use more appropriate language?"

She just shrugged. "Maybe you are. So I'll say it for you. That. Was. A total. Shit. Show."

I did give in to the need to curse, then. I mean, nothing was stopping me.

The guy we'd been interviewing had already left the room, sweating and still probably shaking from the experience of interviewing with us, and the next guy wasn't due for at least ten minutes.

"A shit show," I agreed. "Worse than that, if there is such a thing."

She pursed her lips. "So that makes zero for ten, by my count. Unless I'm missing something."

"You're not. That was our tenth interview. And the tenth completely wrong person."

The truth was, it wasn't even a contest. There was no gray area here. No mistakes being made. No *Maybe we can make this person work if we change some things*. We had gone through the resumes with a fine-toothed comb, just to make sure we were only accepting the best of them and had ended up with twenty candidates who seemed like they might actually be really good. Smart, talented, and they all had great references.

And I'd thought twenty had been enough applicants that we were sure to find someone. Hell, I was thinking we'd probably find more than one someone and have to make a really hard decision. I didn't want Jonathan to leave, but I was optimistic about finding someone great to replace him—and doing it in time for him to start their training before he and his wife took off on their tour of the world.

That was three days ago. Now we were finished with ten of those interviews, and we'd found... nothing.

I mean, worse than nothing. The people we'd been interviewing were actually making me start to wonder about the state of the rest of the business world. Was *everyone* working with this low level of talent out there?

If they were, how the hell was the world still spinning?

"How long do we think Jonathan is going to hang on?" I asked, resting my head in my hands and trying to remember who else we had coming in.

"I think we'll be able to keep him for another week, max," she said quickly. "I know Molly well enough to know that she's not going to be patient for much longer. She's always thought you worked him too hard. Now that she has a chance to get him away from you…"

"She's not going to be generous," I agreed. "Though I didn't think we worked him *that* hard."

She gave me a pointed look. "Leo, you work everyone that hard. It's a multibillion-dollar company. It's a big job." Then she started shuffling through the stack of papers she'd pulled out of her magical notebook and handed one to me. "And that doesn't really matter, anyhow, because the next applicant is going to be here in about five minutes. Study up. Let's see if we can find a way to get this one through the entire interview, at least."

Get him through the entire interview. Right. That seemed like a reasonable goal.

· · ᦉ · ·

"THIS," I TOLD JACK bluntly, "might be what hell is like."

"Hell is a place where you can't find a lead accountant?" he asked, looking scandalized. "That is so weird. I always thought it was a place with no women and all men, so you were bored all the time and couldn't get a decent conversation. Definitely couldn't get laid."

I shook my head at him, torn between laughing and groaning. How very like Jack to make hell about sex.

Not that it was a surprise. He definitely lived his life that way.

I finally decided on groaning, though, because this was serious. This was business. It wasn't a laughing matter.

"The problem is," I continued firmly, "we need someone now. I don't have time to go through another stack of resumes, and even if I did, I've already called the best of them in. If we go through again, I'll be calling in the second team. The not-as-good applicants. And you know how I feel about that."

He dropped into the chair behind his desk and shook his head. "Too right I know how you feel about that, you competitive bastard."

"I'm a good businessman," I retorted. "That requires a competitive spirit."

Jack just rolled his eyes. "And that is why you run this company and I don't."

I dropped into a seat across from him. "My dad started this company, Jack, and I took it over. *That* is why I run this company and you don't. You don't have the right last name. Or the right business sense. If you were running the place, you'd probably sell it to the first pretty girl who made an offer on it."

He didn't even try to argue with me. He just grinned.

"So what's the problem?" he asked. "None of the applicants are good enough for the mighty Folley?"

"None of them are even close," I confirmed. "And we're going to run out of time. I want Jonathan to train the new hire before he leaves, and I don't think we can hold him much longer."

"You're the big businessman here. Don't you know anyone who can step in until you find someone permanent? Someone who can be a sort of... I don't know, pinch hitter? An in-between? A patch?"

I opened my mouth to tell him that if I knew someone like that, I would have already called them to have them step in before Jonathan was actually gone. Because of course it was the ideal answer. Have someone step in to do the job in the short term while I found someone who could take it on longer term. Someone who could do a good enough job for right now and was immediately available.

Wait.

Immediately available as in she was literally living under my roof.

"Olivia," I said quietly.

"What?" Jack asked, his face creased in surprise. "What about her?"

"Olivia," I said more loudly. "Shit, it's perfect. She's some sort of math genius disguised as a girl who lives in her car. I had some work at the apartment yesterday because I needed to figure out what was wrong with the numbers, and she took one look and solved the entire problem in the space of about thirty seconds."

The creases in Jack's face grew even deeper. "Thirty seconds? She's better at numbers than you?"

"Well, I don't know about that," I said.

Though I thought she just might be. I'd been worrying at that problem for a full day, and she'd solved it like it was a kindergarten addition question.

But I wasn't about to admit that to Jack, who would never let me forget it.

"Does she have an education?" he asked.

"Something about business, I think," I said, remembering a piece of conversation about a university she shared with... Who had that been? Linda, the saleswoman, I remembered. Olivia had said that Linda had gone to the same university she had but had majored in something slightly different. They'd gone out to lunch, supposedly to discuss the difference between a marketing degree and an...

"An accounting degree," I said vaguely. "She said she was in school for an accounting degree. But I have no idea if she finished or not. She doesn't exactly seem like she's been working in any high-up accounting job."

"But she could if she wanted to," Jack said quickly. "Theoretically. I mean, it sounds like she has at least some of the education for it."

"She definitely does," I said, feeling excitement starting to grow in my stomach. "And she's got to be the brightest woman I've ever met in my entire life."

Jack gave me shooter fingers and winked—like he was the one who'd come up with the idea.

Although I guessed he sort of was.

"Then it sounds like she's your girl."

I bit my lip, my mind racing. My girl. Well, she definitely wasn't that. Not even close.

But if I could convince her to step in at the office for the short term, to cover the gap between Jonathan leaving and someone else coming on board...

And if it meant she stayed a little bit longer...

And I continued to protect her from whoever I was starting to think she was running from...

It wasn't a good idea. I mean, probably not. I was already having enough trouble keeping my hands off her in the apartment. I wanted her more than I'd ever wanted any other girl I barely knew who happened to be living in my house, and it was getting harder and harder to keep those wants to myself. Especially when I thought she might be starting to want the same thing.

But I might be able to do it for a little bit longer, if it meant keeping the accounting department intact.

And if she was the only choice available to me...

Did I really have any choice?

CHAPTER 17

OLIVIA

"ARE YOU TELLING ME that I have to get *more* clothes?" I asked sharply that night over dinner.

Leo shrugged. "Did you happen to get a brilliant, expensive dress that qualifies as formal evening wear or ball gown when the saleswoman brought clothes before?"

I frowned. "I didn't exactly get a list of requirements when she brought the entire store to the apartment and made me try it all on."

"Okay, that's my fault," he said, cringing. "Although you did know that we were going to a charity auction. I assumed that you would realize from the name that it was... well, important. Dressy."

"Uh-huh. If you needed me to have something specific, you really could have told me so. More efficient. And here I thought you ran an entire company all by yourself."

"I would never claim to run it all by myself," he said seriously. "I have lots and lots of help."

"So next time, maybe I should talk to your assistant?" I smiled charmingly at him to take the sting out of what I'd just said, realizing after I said it that it sounded... well, awfully snarky, to be honest, when the guy had already bought me an entire wardrobe and was now evidently going to buy me even more stuff.

I was going to have a bear of a time fitting it all into my car when it came time to leave. I grimaced at the thought, because it was followed by something else: I might have to leave something behind.

Look, I'm not a materialistic person, usually. My dad might have been rich—or at least I thought he probably was, given what I was guessing he did—but he'd never passed one red penny down to us, and my mom had worked her tiny little butt off keeping us fed and sheltered. I hadn't had any choice but to be grateful for every pair of too-small sneakers and too-short jeans I had.

The idea of materialism had never even crossed my mind.

Which meant I'd never had as many beautiful clothes as I had right now, sitting in the closet in the room that wasn't mine, in the apartment that wasn't mine, courtesy of the guy I barely knew.

Yeah, okay, it sounded really screwed up. But I didn't want to have to leave any of those beautiful clothes behind. I liked having them.

I hated that I liked having them. But that didn't change the feeling.

So when it came to getting another beautiful dress...

"I guess I can be convinced to get something else," I said, forcing myself to sound like I was doing him some major favor.

He made a face at me that said he definitely saw exactly what I was doing. "That's so kind of you. Do you want a credit card?"

I held a hand up to stop him. "I said I'd get a dress, but I will draw the line at actually carrying your credit card around. I'm not a kept woman."

I refrained from noting that at the moment, I was definitely a kept woman. I was living in his house, on his dime, and doing nothing but promising to attend some big events with him.

I mean, technically there was a trade-off. It just... wasn't equal. And I still hadn't figured out exactly why he was being so nice.

I also knew that part of the reason I was acting so pissy right now was that this dress—this event—meant that we were getting very close to the end of the contract we'd agreed upon. After all, the charity auction was what I was here for.

Once that was done, I was going to be free to go. Free to leave this slice of heaven, where I'd felt so safe and well-fed for the last week.

But I didn't think we needed to go through any of that. I definitely didn't think talking about it was going to change anything.

He wasn't exactly going to ask me to stay longer, just from the goodness of his heart. A contract satisfied was a contract satisfied. Period.

"How are you going to get a dress if you don't have a card?" he asked, acting like it was the simplest question in the world.

Luckily, I had a simple answer.

"Easy. You have an account with Linda's store, right? So I'll call my good friend Linda and have her bring over some options. And while she's here, she can give me advice on what looks best. After all, I wouldn't want to embarrass you while we're at this fancy shindig."

I grinned at him, then pulled my phone out and typed Linda's number into the text box.

It wasn't that I was looking forward to spending more of his money. It definitely wasn't that I was looking forward to dressing up for him.

That shiver of excitement that ran up my spine at the thought of making myself pretty and impressing him? The glimmer of heat that bloomed between my legs at the thought of his eyes roving up and down my body as I strutted out in some form-fitting red number?

The way my breath got suddenly shorter, my body starting to feel like liquid sex?

That didn't mean a damn thing. It was just a side effect of knowing that I was going to buy something pretty.

Seriously.

.. ✦ ..

"THIS ONE," LINDA PURRED, pulling a red, sequined, full-length dress out of a garment bag. She turned to me, her face actually shining, and bit her lip. "It's the most gorgeous thing we have in the entire store, and I've been dying to see it on someone, but no one has been able to pull it off."

She stood back and eyed me closely, her eyes slightly narrowed.

"What?" I asked, my eyes snapping between her and the dress in question, which was still folded over her arm. I hadn't even seen it yet, but I already knew I wanted it. It was a ruby color like nothing I'd ever seen before, and I already knew it was going to make my dark hair flash.

So why was she hesitating?

"Am I too short for it or something?"

She shook her head, her bottom lip caught in her teeth in excitement. "I don't think so. I was just thinking about how your curves were going to look in it. You're. Going to be. Gorgeous. We'll need tall shoes, but I brought a bunch with me."

I looked past her at the stack of additional boxes and bags she had. "Is all of that shoes?"

"No," she giggled. "I brought a bunch of other dresses, too. I just don't think you're going to want to bother with them once you've seen this one."

"Then stop teasing me and give it here!" I said, giving her grabby hands.

Her giggling increased, and she handed the dress over, sliding the slinky, gorgeous material over my arm and then turning me and shoving me toward the bedroom. "Get dressed. I'll find shoes."

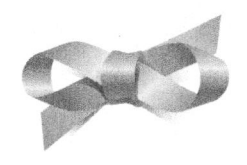

CHAPTER 18

LEO

"YOU LOOK TERRIBLE."

I gave her a very jaded look over the rims of my glasses, not sure exactly how to respond to that at first.

I didn't think anyone had ever said anything like that to me in my entire life. Even when I was in college and staying up until all hours studying, no one had actually ever gone out of their way to tell me I looked terrible.

Then again, I'd never met anyone like Olivia Cadwell, who seemed to be three times as straightforward as any normal human being.

I hated to admit it, but I kind of loved that about her.

"Thanks," I said drily. "You, on the other hand, look like a million bucks."

She flashed me a charming, brilliant smile and seated herself at the breakfast table. "What are we having? And why are you looking so fatigued and stressed?"

I pushed the bag of bagels toward her, followed by the tub of cream cheese. "Bagels and cream cheese. I had them delivered this morning, so they're fresh. And I look like I haven't slept in days because I actually haven't slept in days."

A frown shot across her face. "Why not? Why didn't you say anything?"

Now that was rich. This girl had been bouncing back and forth between coming on to me and ignoring me and she wondered why I hadn't what, knocked on her door in the middle of the night and asked if she felt like a movie and some popcorn?

"I didn't exactly think you were the having-a-chat-in-the-middle-of-the-night sort of girl," I told her honestly. "I haven't been sleeping well because we've got a problem at work. My head accountant quit, and though he said he'd stay on to train the new hire, I'm having more trouble than I would have thought possible finding a new hire. The only guy I liked even a little bit just took a job with another company. And even he wasn't going to be a stellar employee."

Her mouth quirked. "Why not? Did he not fit the superhero profile?" She gestured vaguely at my body. "Broad shoulders, six-pack, firm jaw..."

I felt the entire world grow still for a moment at her words.

Wait a minute. Had she ever seen my stomach? How did she know I had a six-pack?

Wait again. Was she even talking about *me*?

I cleared my throat, trying to get my brain to unscramble itself at the idea of her staring at my body and get back on track. "Um, no. No superhero there. I thought he might have a brain meltdown during the interview itself, so I'm thinking he's all human."

Her frown was back now. "If he had a meltdown during the interview, what makes you think he's going to be able to handle anything about the job? An accountant at a company that does $3 billion in sales every year, across all the smaller divisions? He's going to have an outright heart attack within the first month."

Now it was my turn to frown. "How do you know how much volume we do?"

She tipped her head toward me. "It's this thing called Google. You might have heard of it."

"You looked up my company?"

She just shrugged. "I wanted to see who you were. I also assumed you'd done the same thing to me, so it felt like fair play."

Now I wondered if she somehow knew that Jack had suggested I hire a PI.

She knew about my six-pack. She knew that my best friend was suggesting I do research on her. What was this girl, a psychic?

"I haven't," I said sharply. Too sharply.

It was the statement of a guilty conscience. I knew that much. I was hoping, though, that she didn't see it that way.

"But you're right. We didn't get any good applicants, and I'm afraid I'm out of time with Jonathan. His wife wants to do some trip around the world, and she's not going without him, and I've heard she's already bought the tickets, so it's not like we can drag this out forever."

"Sounds like a smart woman," she said. "So you need a replacement, and you're out of time, and no one seems to be fitting the bill. Well, I'd say the answer is right in front of your face."

I stared at her, completely lost. "I'm sorry, what?"

She snorted. "Typical man. You're so busy worrying about how you're going to handle something that you don't even bother to look around you. It's easy. You need an accountant. I happen to be really, really good with numbers. I'll take care of things for you until you can find a replacement. Simple."

I'd always read about people whose mouths fell open when they heard something surprising, and I'd never really believed it could actually happen until that moment, when my mouth did indeed fall open.

I realized a split second later that I probably looked like a complete idiot, though, and snapped it shut again.

"You?" I asked.

It was so close to what Jack and I had talked about that I wondered again whether she had some way to listen in on what I did in the office.

Which... felt a whole lot like something else she'd said about secretly spying on my company and selling the information.

Shit, was she actually some sort of corporate spy here on the most bizarre con ever?

You are actually losing it, son, a voice inside my head said coldly. *Since when did you start thinking things like that?*

Since Olivia Cadwell casually fell into my life—by nearly running me over—and charmed me by not wanting anything to do with me, while being so obviously in need of help, I thought.

And while being the sexiest, most interesting woman I'd ever met in my life.

One who treated me like any other guy, rather than the billionaire she was trying to land.

"So let me get this straight," I said. "You're not only an accountant, but also one that thinks she can handle the pressure of a multibillion-dollar company that does $3 billion in sales every year. Not only that, but you think you can handle the lead job in the accounting department."

She made a face. "I mean, I'm not a certified accountant, but I've got three years of school under my belt. And I'm better with numbers than anyone I've ever met. It also doesn't sound like you've got much choice."

I didn't. She was definitely right about that.

And I'd seen her capability with numbers.

It also hadn't escaped my attention that the charity ball was this weekend, which meant that as of Sunday, our contract would be over. She'd be leaving.

And I didn't know if I'd ever see her again. Because I really, really doubted she'd give me a forwarding number. I also didn't think she'd stay any longer than we'd agreed to. Sure, she probably liked having the apartment to come home to. And access to food. And hot water.

But she'd never been anything but honest about her plans. She'd been reminding me since she arrived that she'd be leaving as soon as the charity auction was over.

It took me about two seconds to realize that I didn't want her to go. I didn't know exactly what I wanted with her yet—or what I might be able to ask from her—but I knew that I wanted more time to figure that out.

I wasn't ready to let her go.

And she was offering me the perfect way to keep her in my house for a little bit longer. I didn't know whether I had feelings for the girl, and I didn't know if she had any feelings for me, but I knew that I wanted a little bit more time before I had to say goodbye.

"Deal," I said firmly. "I'm leaving in about half an hour. How quickly can you be ready to go in?"

CHAPTER 19

OLIVIA

I HAVE TO SAY, FROM what Leo had said, I went into his office thinking that I was going into the battle of my life or something. The entire way there, he filled my head full of the importance of the position, the size of the company itself, the number of employees, and the revenue of each department.

He even gave me a breakdown of the smaller companies existing under the umbrella of the larger corporation.

It didn't take me long to figure out that he'd memorized almost everything to do with the entire corporation and was really pretty good at numbers himself.

And he still hadn't been able to figure out what was wrong with that one batch of paperwork he'd given me. Really, it almost had me believing him when he insisted that this position was difficult and would require every single ounce of my brainpower.

When I got there, of course, it turned out that it actually only took about *half* my brainpower.

I met the infamous Jonathan and got a quick breakdown of what the position required and how the department ran, and from there we walked through the tasks I'd be taking over, where the numbers I came up with would go, and how I needed to check them to make sure they were as correct as they could be before they were passed on to whoever was receiving them. I got access to all the accounts—after I signed the appropriate NDAs, of course, because heaven forbid I take their information and sell it to the highest bidder, whoever that might be—and learned the accounting software they used to track everything. I even got access to the network where they stored the spreadsheets with every employee's spending accounts.

It took me the morning to learn everything Jonathan claimed I would need to know, though he'd promised me it would take at least a week to get up to speed.

It took me an hour after that to start locating the errors they'd been making in their everyday tasks. Another hour and I'd refined half of their most important systems so they'd be not only more efficient but also more accurate.

"It'll save the company a ton of money in billable hours, and even more in revenue that's just falling into the cracks," I told Jonathan as I showed him what I'd come up with.

I could feel the amazed stare coming from him, though I didn't turn my face to see it. I did grin a little bit, though, and I'm not even ashamed to admit that.

"You are going to be good," he said, his voice full of admiration. "Where the hell did he find you?"

"Sleeping in my car in the alley right below us," I said primly. "He thought I looked like I might know numbers, and I have to admit, he was right. Can you point me toward the bathroom? And also, coffee. I require caffeine, stat."

He just pointed, his brain—and probably his tongue—being too stunned by what I'd just said to really come up with an answer.

I walked away grinning, so overjoyed to be using my brain again to care whether he actually believed me or not. Who would it hurt, really, to tell the truth, after all? It wasn't like anyone else around here knew what I actually was to Leo. No one would realize that I was living in his house or planning to go to the charity function with him, or that I was here in his office as a favor to him—though he would never in a million years realize it, I didn't think.

After all, he was the one who liked playing knight in shining armor. I didn't think he'd ever even consider that someone else might be saving *him*.

I also didn't think he'd ever think I was doing it because I was very quickly starting to wish I was more than just a girl he'd hired to be his date to some fancy party. At least I hoped not. Because I already had enough on my plate.

I didn't need to deal with any sticky emotional ties on top of it.

• • ⁂ • •

"JONATHAN TELLS ME THAT you're a phenom and that I'd be stupid to ever let you go," Leo said, taking a sip of his wine and grinning at me over the salads he'd ordered us at a restaurant I already knew was way too fancy for a midweek meal.

Look, I was a burgers-and-fries sort of girl. I could do dressier places, but it certainly wasn't the speed I liked in my life.

I'd had to wear a skirt out to dinner tonight—and heels—and as far as I was concerned, that meant I'd gotten awfully dressed up just to eat.

The wine, though, was amazingly good. And I figured that could make up for a whole lot.

I took another sip of it and let the liquid roll over my tongue, all blackberries and oak. Then I gave him the grin and nod I knew he was expecting.

"I have to say, I am pretty good," I admitted. "Though I'm afraid you're not going to have much choice about letting me go. And we both know it."

He bit his lip, his face going very serious, but quickly returned to the playful expression he'd been wearing a moment ago. "Well, we'll just have to see about that, won't we?" he asked. "Now, enough about work. We're not in the office anymore, and that means I don't want to talk about the office. Tell me something else, instead. Tell me a story from your childhood."

I kept the grimace from my face, but just barely. Tell him about my childhood? Yeah, that sounded like a terrific idea. Tell the man who had everything about the childhood of someone who hadn't exactly been on the run from the law but had definitely been on the run from the bill collectors. Tell him about the girl who hadn't known her father but suspected that she knew who he was—and from there, tell him that I thought I was probably luckier to be out from under the thumb of someone I thought was probably pretty high up in New York's mafia.

Tell him about my mother, who'd barely been able to keep a roof over our heads. Tell him about wearing clothes that were a size too small because we couldn't afford new ones when I grew.

Tell him about running from said mother's new boyfriend, who had threatened my life when I tried to stand up for her.

No, thank you.

He had the most adorably expectant look on his face, though, just waiting for something personal, and so I started thumbing through my memories, looking for things that would make him happy... without giving away too much of my identity.

"When I was little, I'd go outside and look specifically for ladybugs," I told him quietly, smiling at the memory—which was real. "Just because I'd hear that they could bring you good luck, and I knew I needed some. Every time I found one, I'd run screaming back into the house with it to show my mom."

He chuckled. "And did they change your luck?"

Definitely not. We'd still been broke, and my mother had still continued to date losers. My dad still hadn't sent any money to help out.

"You know, I don't know," I said, brushing past the thought I'd had. "But I like to think they did. Now you."

And so started a game where we told each other random pieces of trivia—either memories from our childhoods or things we'd picked up along the way that felt like they might come in handy.

And as we talked, we drank. And when dinner came, we continued to drink. And dessert... Yep, more drinking.

Which was how we ended up getting into his car at the end of the night, both of us nearly incapable of taking a straight step on our own. The truth was, I think I actually fell into the back of his car rather than just sitting down.

I clutched at my skirt and pulled it back down from where it had ridden up my legs, suddenly conscious of just how much I was showing, and glanced up, hoping against hope that he hadn't seen.

No such luck, of course. His eyes were on my legs and all the skin I was showing.

And when he turned them back up to me, they were asking all sorts of questions I wasn't sure I was in any position to answer. Questions about us and what we were doing. Why we were out to dinner on a weeknight, both of us dressed up and drinking too much wine.

Why, exactly, we were spending hours and hours over a meal that should have taken one, tops... and why I was feeling a whole lot like it was the best date of my entire life. Even though it hadn't been.

Based on the look he was wearing, I was guessing he'd thought it was a pretty good night, too.

I was also guessing he wanted to see whether it was going to keep going. The problem was, I wasn't sure whether I wanted to take this any further... or run as quickly as I could manage in the other direction before someone ended up getting hurt.

　　　＊　＊　＊

WE STUMBLED OUT OF the elevator and into his apartment, both of us laughing at our inability to walk responsibly, and the heels I'd been wearing took that stumble as an excuse to turn traitor. Instead of straightening out from the initial bobble and continuing on, my ankles both twisted to the side, sending me quickly toward the floor.

A pair of hands shot under my arms and caught me, though, and before I knew it, I was not only back on my feet but shoved up against the wall next to the elevator, Leo up against me and his face entirely too close.

"What are you doing?" I asked breathlessly.

Needlessly, honestly, as I knew exactly what he was doing. I might have had an entire bottle of wine to drink. That didn't make me stupid.

"Exactly what I've been wanting to do all night," he whispered back.

And he used his body to pin me to the wall, slid his hands up my neck and into my hair, and pulled it loose from the fancy updo I'd created just for the night. When it came down, all curled and messy, he threaded his fingers through the curls, biting his lip and staring at them.

And then his eyes came back to me, hot and wet and wanting.

"I've wanted to kiss you all night," he murmured. "I've wanted to kiss you for a week."

I'd been wanting the same thing. I just hadn't admitted it to myself until right then.

"Then I guess you'd better get to it," I whispered.

It started gently. Just a brush of his lips against mine, the softest touch of his thumbs against my neck. But the moment I lifted my chin up to take more of him in, my blood rushing so hot and fast through my veins that I didn't think I could stop myself, it suddenly turned rougher. Within seconds, he was using his hand on my jaw to force my mouth even wider, pushing himself against me even harder, his hips rocking with need.

And I was pushing back. Rocking with him. Spreading my legs as far as they would go in that stupid skirt, the space between my legs buzzing with a desperate desire to have him there.

Fuck, I wanted the man. Wanted him worse than I thought I'd ever wanted anything in my entire life. And it wasn't just about this moment. It was about a whole lot more than that. The solid, safe feel of him at my side. The knowledge that if something happened, he'd be standing behind me, waiting to catch me.

The feel of his desire singing through our connection.

It was like nothing I'd ever felt before, and though I'd been trying hard to fight it for the last week, I realized now that I wasn't going to be able to do it. Not even a little bit.

His lips left my own, my mouth still singing with the taste of him, and went to my neck, rougher now as they kissed and sucked their way down my skin. He moved his fingers from my hair to the neck of my shirt, busy at the buttons, but I could already tell that it wasn't going to be quick enough.

I wanted him now. I didn't want to wait for anything slow or sensual or polite.

"Leo," I started, ready to tell him just to rip the stupid thing off.

But he'd already grabbed both sides of the blouse and torn it right down the middle, his hands going immediately inside the silk to cup my breasts, and I pushed against him with a gasp, the rest of my statement lost.

"Fuck," he groaned. "You have no idea how badly I've been wanting to touch you for the last week."

"Probably as bad as I've been wanting to touch you," I murmured, my breath hot and fast at what his fingers were doing.

Damn, this man was good. He'd already undone my bra and taken both nipples in his fingers, and the thing he was doing with his tongue underneath my ear was...

"Fuck," I gasped. "Leo."

"Too much?" he whispered against my skin.

"Not... enough..." I returned, barely able to speak.

That seemed to be some sort of sign, too, because his fingers suddenly moved, leaving my nipples cold and pebbled in the cool air, and a second later, he was yanking my skirt up, exposing my legs... and then my thong. He continued to yank until my skirt was circling my waist, leaving my entire lower half nearly bare.

Then he spread my legs even further and reared back to look at me. "Too much?" he asked, his voice tense with desire.

I bit my lip and shook my head. At this point, the man could throw me over the back of the couch and have his way with me and it still wouldn't be too much. I was nearly melting from his touch, my desire growing so quickly that I thought I might explode the first time he—

He slid his fingers between my legs so suddenly that I didn't even see him move, and the feel of his fingertips spreading me apart made me gasp and nearly collapse with sudden pleasure.

He caught me with one strong hand and moved forward to press me against the wall with his body again... and then proceeded to start circling my clit with his fingertips, brushing and stroking until I was vibrating with need.

I threw my face up and moved with him, praying he'd go further. Praying he didn't mean to tease me for much longer. And when it started to look like he was going to tease me for as long as he damn well wanted, I started begging.

That's right. I'm not even afraid to admit it.

"Damn, Leo, please," I gasped. "Stop teasing. Please. I can't stand it."

I could feel his lips smiling as they pressed against my neck. "You're not nearly as stubborn as I thought you were," he murmured.

He picked me up, moved three steps to get to the table next to us, and shoved everything off the table. A moment later, I was sitting on the table, open and vulnerable to him, and he was sliding my panties to the side. Another quick move and his own pants dropped to the floor.

And here he had me at a disadvantage, because though he'd seen me naked—or nearly naked—I hadn't seen one single inch of him.

And he was glorious. Every single inch of him.

"Like what you see?" he murmured.

I looked up at him and matched the grin he was wearing. "I do. The question is whether you know how to use it."

He leaned toward me, stepping in between my legs and forcing them even wider, then picking them up and bending my knees so that my feet were on the table, my center completely exposed.

"I'll prove it to you," he whispered, staring into my eyes.

I felt the head of his cock nudge my opening and caught my breath.

And then he put his hands to my hips and held me still while he sheathed himself in me, holding me there as he began to move in and out so slowly that it made me want to scream with the need for more.

When he finally did give me more—harder and faster and deeper than I could have imagined possible—I did start screaming. And I didn't care who heard me.

CHAPTER 20

LEO

I FELT HER NEXT TO me before I even opened my eyes the next morning, a warm weight that I had curled around at some point in the night when I wasn't even aware of it.

My lips curved into a very satisfied, very comfortable smile, and I wrapped my arms around her and pulled her deeper into the curve of my body, wanting to be able to feel her with every single inch of my skin.

She moaned sleepily and moved around a bit, finding a more comfortable position. Then she fell back into a doze, which was perfect as it gave me time to think before I got around to having the conversation we were inevitably going to have to have when she woke all the way up.

Because I wasn't kidding myself about that part. I'd known Olivia only a week, and I already knew that she didn't let things go by without some sort of comment or opinion. She always had an opinion. And she almost never kept it to herself.

The truth was, it was one of the things I liked best about her. Hey, you live a life where you've been rich and highly sought after since you were born, and tell me how much you trust the people around you to tell you the truth.

That's right. You won't trust them at all, because you'll have learned when you were young that they'll say anything that they think will make you do what they want or like them better. And you'll turn out just like me.

The sort of person who treasures honesty more than almost anything else in the world.

So when a girl shows up, nearly hits you with a car, and then acts like she's totally uninterested in you, you'll probably find it the most alluring thing in the world. Just like I did.

And that didn't even start on the way she looked when she smiled. Those sparkling, laughing eyes that changed from blue to green and back again, depending on her mood. The tiny, curvy body that fit just right up against me...

I felt myself growing hard again at the thought of it and closed my mouth on the groan that wanted to come with the sensation. I'd had her three times last night—after the first time in the entryway—and it still hadn't been enough.

The truth was, I didn't know if it would *ever* be enough.

Not that I had any right to think anything like that. As far as I knew, nothing had changed. Olivia was most likely still planning to leave just as soon as she felt like she'd fulfilled her end of the deal. Officially, that was the night of the charity auction.

Now that she was working in my office, though, and in a position where I desperately needed someone, I was thinking I might be able to convince her to extend her stay.

If she continued to perform as well in the office as she had yesterday, I didn't know if I could stand to let her go. Hell, after last night, I didn't know if I could stand to let her go.

Not that I could tell her that. Something told me that saying such things would be the quickest way to get her to run in the opposite direction.

And there was also that little matter of needing to know exactly who she was and where she'd come from.

I almost groaned again at that thought, every ounce of lust abruptly leaving my body. Because none of this was going to matter if she was keeping secrets that actually mattered, rather than just things she didn't want to talk about.

I took the thought, shoved it in a closet in my head, and locked the door on it. I'd think about that later.

Right now, I wanted to think about only two things. First, waking Olivia up, and second, making love to her again.

I knew it was only a matter of time until I had to get serious about figuring out who she was. But right now, for this one moment, I was going to take advantage of not needing to know. I pressed my lips softly to the back of her neck, allowing my tongue to dart out and taste her skin, and moved my fingers up to one nipple, beginning to play with it in the hopes of waking her up.

· · ∞ · ·

THE FIRST ITEM ON MY schedule that morning was a meeting with Jack—which at this point seemed most fortuitous.

"Cancel the ad for a new accountant," I told him the moment he walked into my office. "We don't need one anymore."

He stopped short, shocked. "Why? Are we getting rid of the accounting department? Going to fly by the seat of our pants and just hope for the best? I'm the CFO, Leo. Don't you think I should have been in on a decision like that?"

I snorted. "You know me too well to think that, Jack. I never fly by the seat of my pants when it comes to business. But I've already filled the position."

Jack's frown deepened. "You have? Again, I have to say... CFO. Should be involved in things like hiring new people."

"And yet I've already hired her and she's on her second day of work, and you weren't involved in any way."

Another moment of frowning, and then Jack's expression suddenly cleared. "The girl from the car? Is she the one you're talking about?"

I shuffled through some papers on my desk, desperate for something to do that didn't include looking right at Jack when I said the next line. "She sure is. She's brilliant, Jack, and she doesn't even have to try. I've decided that I'm keeping her."

He smirked. "That sounds like it means you're keeping her in more than one way. Did something happen between you two?"

Something had happened. Lots of somethings had happened—repeatedly. I was still sporting the scratches—and a semi—that proved exactly what had happened between us.

But that was none of Jack's business, and I knew him well enough to know that if I so much as mentioned having taken her to bed last night, it would be blasted across the entire company by the end of the day. Right now, no one knew anything but that I had found a new accountant.

As far as I was concerned, that was how it was going to stay. For everyone's good.

"She's the best fit for the job, Jack," I said, meeting his eyes. "And I like having the best people around me. That's all there is to it."

He narrowed his eyes like he was going to argue with me on that point but then nodded. Evidently, he'd realized that he wouldn't get anywhere with that argument.

"If you're keeping her, you know you're going to have to actually find out what her background is," he said seriously, all joking gone. "If she's not going to tell you, then you're going to have to hire a PI. I know you don't want to do it, Leo, but..."

"I know," I said, cutting him off.

He didn't have to tell me. I wasn't going to argue with him about it anymore. I'd come to the realization this morning over breakfast, and though I'd given myself several hours to think about it, I hadn't changed my mind.

It was one thing to hire the girl to be my date to a big party. Even having her in my house hadn't been a big deal. I'd been willing to let her stay a stranger under those circumstances.

But now I was talking about keeping her on in the company. She'd have access to everything. And I couldn't just approve that without having more information about who she was and where she'd come from.

I also couldn't keep falling for her without even knowing whether Olivia was her real name. Though I didn't think I'd better bring that up to the PI... or to Jack.

I was going to have enough trouble explaining to them how I'd fallen for the girl I'd found living in her car in the alley outside my building in the first place.

CHAPTER 21

OLIVIA

"HAVE I TOLD YOU HOW freaking nervous I am about this?" I asked—not for the first time—as we sat eating breakfast and reading the paper.

He had the business section. I had the news. Once we were finished with our sections, we'd switch. It was something we'd started doing sometime during the week, though I didn't really remember when. And now that I thought about it... I didn't even remember any discussion around this move.

It had just sort of... happened.

Sort of like how it had just happened that we'd slept together two nights ago. After spending hours and hours over a fancy dinner and too much wine. After I'd agreed to start working at his office, to save him from losing any more sleep over the fact that he didn't have a lead accountant.

Yeah, things were starting to get really, really twisty. And I was completely losing my hold on that whole no-emotions thing I'd promised myself I'd be maintaining when it came to Leo Folley and the deal we'd made together.

Which meant it was a pretty good thing I'd be leaving soon, I realized. The sooner I got through tonight and got the hell out of here, the sooner I could get around to forgetting about this guy. And the world he'd introduced me to. And the safety I felt whenever I was around him.

"You've mentioned it," he said, glancing up and giving me a quick glimpse of that grin he was starting to wear so often. "Which is exactly why I figured you wouldn't want to leave the house today. More inside time during the day might give you more energy for tonight. You think?"

I hadn't thought of it that way, but now that he said it, the idea of staying in all day in preparation for the charity auction tonight... did make a certain amount of sense.

"I like it," I said. "But what am I supposed to do all locked up by myself all day?"

I half thought he'd say something clever, like that he'd be giving me something to do—not that I wanted anything like that from him, since I was officially Not Interested—but instead, he surprised me with something else. "I've got people coming over to do your hair, nails, and makeup, actually," he said, going back to his paper. "Figured you might like the help, too."

He said it in such a casual way that it sounded like he'd barely planned anything at all. Like it was some sort of throwaway comment.

The self-satisfied smile creeping across his lips told me otherwise.

I reached out and took another bagel off the pile he always seemed to keep around. "And I'm guessing you just came up with that right now, huh? No planning at all?"

The smile on his face grew. "None whatsoever," he said, refusing to look away from his paper. "I just happened to think of it right now."

I spread cream cheese across a piece of bagel and lifted one eyebrow in his general direction. "Pretty amazing that they're available on such short notice."

He finally looked up at me and quirked a brow of his own. "Isn't it, though?"

And at that, I laughed, suddenly too amused by him to worry about what tonight was and what it would bring. Too charmed by him randomly scheduling a mani/pedi, as well as hair and makeup, to think about the fact that tonight would be our last night together.

Because after this charity auction, our contract was at an end.

Which meant that after tonight, I'd be leaving this gorgeous apartment—and the gorgeous man it housed—behind me.

I didn't like the thought. So I sent it away the moment I'd had it and told it not to come back until tomorrow.

· · ⚜ · ·

THE DAY PASSED IN A whirl of colors and women, all of them mixed up together like we were all in some enormous crayon box, and by the time the evening rolled around and I realized it was actually time to start thinking about getting dressed, I not only had bright red fingernails and toes, but also better makeup than I'd ever worn in my entire life.

It was so good, in fact, that looking into the mirror was a whole lot like looking at a stranger.

"Money really does buy you anything, I guess," I said, turning my face back and forth to look at the job Maria, the hair and makeup person, had done.

I could barely recognize myself, and I was positive that no one back home would have recognized me in this particular getup. Maybe I should have thought about using makeup as a disguise before I was actually doing it.

Because I had to face it. This entire thing—the makeup, the nails, the fancy updo with several curls hanging down—was nothing more than a disguise. One that was meant to get me through tonight and a whole load of fancy people that I wouldn't know how to talk to.

And if I was lucky, one that would hide my identity from anyone who happened to look at any pictures that might be taken of me tonight.

Shit, I hoped there weren't photographers. I hoped I could get through the entire night without embarrassing myself or Leo. I hoped I could get through the night without jumping his bones and dragging him into the closest bathroom.

No. I couldn't think that way. I was only here through tonight, and then this entire adventure was over. That was the only thing that mattered here. Leo hadn't exactly asked me to stay any longer, and as far as I could see, that meant he was just as ready for the whole charade to be over as I was.

"Get through tonight, and you're done," I told my reflection. "Get through tonight and you're done."

It wasn't the best mantra I'd ever heard. But it was going to have to be good enough.

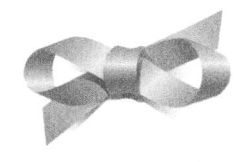

CHAPTER 22

LEO

I'D BEEN OUT OF THE apartment all day, and by the time I got home again, my tux in its garment bag across my arm, fresh from the cleaners, Olivia was already ensconced in her room, getting ready.

I paused in the hallway, my hand raised to knock. I wanted to tell her about my day. Ask about hers. Talk about what we were going to do tonight and start to plan our exit. Maybe even come up with a code word that we could use when we decided we'd had enough and wanted to get out of there.

And those were exactly the kinds of things you did when you were actually with someone. Not the things you did when you wanted to be with someone but were doing everything you could to keep your emotions in check.

For now. Until you knew more about the someone in question.

And that second one? That was where I was. I wanted the girl. Badly. I wanted her to stay on and keep working at the company and keep waking up and having breakfast with me every morning. I wanted midnight snacks and movies and hours spent over fancy dinners with plenty of wine.

Of course, I wanted all of those things with a girl I was sure was actually named Olivia and whose background I knew. And that was why I put my hand back down, took a deep breath, and passed by her door, turning my eyes resolutely to my own suite and my bathroom. I needed a shower, and I needed to make sure this tux still looked as good as I remembered.

I also needed a very firm reminder that Olivia wasn't mine to keep. Not yet.

. . ⚜ . .

BY THE TIME I WAS SHOWERED and powdered (whatever that meant) and dressed, an hour had passed. I walked down the hallway, fastening my watch and remembering how much I disliked the shoes that went best with my tux—someone had evidently thought they didn't need any padding at all—and saw that Olivia's door was now ajar.

It had been closed tightly before.

I felt a little thrill of excitement jump through my limbs, like someone had suddenly taken an electric wire to me, and stopped outside of it.

And there... I paused. Trying once more to get my emotions to slow down and fit into the neat little box I'd designed for them. Trying to remind myself—again—that I didn't know this girl, and I needed to know more about her before I actually let myself feel the things my heart was trying to make me feel.

Right. Strong. Firm. Unemotional.

Those were the words of the day.

Then Olivia opened the door, and those words flew right out of my head.

The woman was... beyond gorgeous. Beyond anything I could have imagined. Her dark hair was done up in the back, though whoever had done it had left a few ringlets out around her face. Her eyes were lined in black and shadowed with dark browns and rich reds, and her lips were red enough to look like they were bleeding.

The dress, meanwhile, was...

"Wow," I breathed, unable to think of anything else to say.

That fabulously red mouth smirked. "Why, thank you," she said, glancing down at the sequined, formfitting red dress and extremely tall shoes she was wearing. "Right back atcha."

When I looked up at her face, dragging my eyes away from the dress itself, I saw that despite the casual, joking tone of voice, she was actually quite flattered that I'd noticed.

She was blushing. And she was beautiful.

"You look more gorgeous than anyone I've ever seen in my life," I said, offering her my arm. "I'm going to have to fight to keep you away from the other men at the auction."

She took my arm and gave me another smile. "Don't worry," she whispered. "I've got a dagger hidden on my thigh. I'll be your backup."

I laughed and walked into the hall, ready for the charity auction and all its photographers and reporters and feeling a whole lot better about the whole thing now that I knew I was going to have Olivia Cadwell there as my backup.

. . ∞ . .

THE AUCTION WAS EVERYTHING I'd expected it to be—partially because I'd been to these sorts of things before.

Olivia, however, was looking around us with something bordering on panic. Which was the only reason I kept her arm looped in mine, her body up against me.

"Are there always this many people?" she asked, her voice wavering a little bit.

I glanced down at the ballroom in front of us, considering her question. The place was packed, yes, all of the people below us wearing formal clothing and lots and lots of jewelry. There were people dancing, too, and people drinking and eating the food the charity had provided.

"Well, there'll be more when the auction actually starts," I said, trying to be fair. "This is just the lead-up to it."

"More?" she asked weakly.

I remembered what she'd said about not being great with people she didn't know and remembered further that she hadn't been brought up in this sort of lifestyle. True, I didn't know what her past held, exactly, but I did know that she came from the country. Her accent told me as much.

Maybe I should have given her more time to get used to the idea of what we were about to do.

"You'll be fine," I told her quickly. I pointed out a group of men near the bar, about ten of them standing around and laughing together in rich voices and even richer clothes. "See those men right there?"

Her eyes swiveled from the dancers to the group I was pointing out, and she nodded. "Yeah."

"Those are the men I have to talk to. Or rather... Well, we have to at least stop by to say hello to them. Get through that, and we'll be home free and I won't make you talk to anyone else for the entire night. Deal?"

She offered me a smile that showed a bit of the sass I'd been coming to know this week.

"And there'll be dancing. And food. And champagne," I added, sweetening the deal with everything I had at my disposal.

The smile grew broader, and her eyes started to flash again.

"And I was also thinking we need a safe word," I continued. "Something we can use for when we're ready to go."

She bubbled with laughter at that, and I suddenly had my Olivia back.

"Armadillo," she said quickly.

I made a face. "Really? Why? Do you secretly love them or something? Wait, do you have them as pets? Is that what you do? You're secretly an armadillo breeder?"

She just shrugged. "When I'm not doing superhero stuff. It's a good word for that sort of thing. Not exactly something that might come up in conversation and confuse you."

"Unless you're at an armadillo convention," I noted.

"If we were at an armadillo convention, I obviously would have said 'lizard' rather than 'armadillo,'" she noted quietly. "Let's go. I want to get through this and get to the dancing."

She led the way down the stairs, and moments later, she was sidling up to the men in the group, saying she'd heard they were friends of mine and that we were here to make our appearance. They all glanced at her, glanced away, and then glanced back, and before long, she had them all laughing and asking her advice on which wine they should buy their wives.

It was a thing of beauty.

Particularly when I knew how uncomfortable she was.

She turned around after about ten minutes, though, widened her eyes, and mouthed "armadillo" at me, her eyes taking on a sort of desperate quality.

Right. Time to play knight in shining armor.

I took her arm and grinned at the group of friends and investors, noting that half of them were looking at her rather than me. A shot of jealousy ran through me, but I pushed it down.

The shot of confidence that followed, that she was with me and not them, was a whole lot more rewarding.

"Gentlemen, I've promised this lady a dance," I told them firmly. "I'm going to take her now, if you don't mind."

A chorus of arguments and refusals chimed out, but I didn't let that stop me from turning her smoothly toward the dance floor and gliding out toward the other couples.

"Oh, well done," she said. "Those guys never even knew what hit them."

"Oh, I had it easy," I murmured. "They were so stunned by you that they didn't even see me coming."

Her laugh was like silvery, tinkling bells as I took one hand and spun her out onto the dance floor, then brought her back toward my body and started swaying slowly.

At that moment, a voice sounded out across the loudspeaker, announcing that the charity had already raised over $15 million and that an anonymous benefactor had donated $10 million of that.

I allowed a small smile of pride to touch my face. The auction hadn't even started yet, and they'd already raised that much. That was very, very good news.

And though I thought I'd been hiding that smile, I'd evidently been wrong. Olivia immediately tipped her head.

"Let me guess," she whispered. "That $10 million that came from an anonymous donor came from someone who happens to be dancing right now."

I gave her a shocked look. "You?"

"You," she said, smiling.

I shrugged. "Maybe. Maybe not." I spun her around, doing several turns, and then pulled her back in. "You, Olivia, are a terrific dancer. I wouldn't have expected it. Dance lessons when you were young?"

"Not even close," she said, her face going awry. "We couldn't afford that sort of thing. But I had a friend who had a dad who liked father/daughter dances. And she wouldn't go with him. So I got to go instead."

I dipped toward her and brushed a soft kiss across her lips, stunned by how easily she'd given up that information... and heartbroken at the look of loss on her face when she told it.

This girl had been hurt by someone. Deserted, maybe. And knowing that made me want to hold her to me and protect her for the rest of my life.

It made me want that so bad that it actually shocked me.

To my surprise, she kissed me back, her body sort of melting into mine, and when I drew back, she was smiling hazily.

"What was that for?"

"A promise," I whispered. "I'll take you dancing as often as you want, if it means I get to see you looking as beautiful as you do tonight."

Her smile got bigger, though I saw a hitch in it that said she'd tried to shut it down.

I didn't pay attention to that, though. I was too busy wondering how long we'd have to stay before I could steal her away back home and back to my bed.

CHAPTER 23

OLIVIA

THE NEXT MORNING, I woke up in that slow, delicious way you wake up when you know you don't have to go anywhere, and you've had quite a lot to drink and your body isn't yet ready to be fully functional.

Then I remembered the other reason I wasn't ready to be fully functional and allowed a sly, satisfied, catlike grin to creep onto my face.

I was sore in the most delicious ways, too, and tired from a night of sex with Leo, and that seemed an equally good reason for lying around in bed.

I turned and saw the man in question lying next to me, his eyes already opened, and I stretched luxuriously, keeping my eyes on him as I did it.

Daring him to do something about my naked body being on display right in front of him.

He smiled at me as well and then moved quickly, pulling me onto him and settling me down on his already hard cock.

I moaned, then grinned lazily and started moving, rocking back and forth in a way that wasn't going to get us anywhere quickly. I was too sore for that. I was too tired.

But hot damn, the feel of him filling me up against so soon, stretching muscles that were already so tender...

"Fuck, you feel good," he murmured, his hands on my hips and his fingers pressing into me.

"Mmmm, good morning to you, too," I murmured. "I could get used to this."

I leaned forward and kissed him gently, my attention divided between his lips and the point where we joined each other. Both equally tender. Both so wonderful that I knew I shouldn't think about them for too long, or I'd risk breaking the pleasure of it.

He finished the kiss and smiled up at me. "The problem is," he said, "I really want a shower."

I glanced out the window, surprised. It was light out, but not so light that I thought we necessarily needed to get up yet. "Already?" I asked. "It's like six in the morning or something."

I paused while I thought about this, and he moved his hands, putting me in motion again. I arched against him, the friction of his body starting to get to me regardless of my soreness and fatigue.

And I started speeding up.

To my surprise, he pulled me off him, though, turned me on my back, and leaned down to kiss me while my body tensed in absolute dissatisfaction.

"I'm meeting my parents for breakfast, and I want you to come with me," he whispered. "But first, we need to have a shower."

The way he said it made me think that he meant a whole lot more than just getting washed, and I smiled up at him. "And am I invited to this shower?"

He spread my legs and brushed his fingers up against my folds, making me jerk with need. "I would be sorely disappointed if you weren't there. Let's go."

• • ৎ৹ঌ • •

I HAD BARELY STEPPED into his enormous shower when he grabbed me, turned me around, and pushed me up against the wall, his chest against my back and his hands on my hips.

"What's this?" I gasped. "I thought we were having a shower?"

He leaned in and bit the shell of my ear gently. "We are. See? The water's running, isn't it?"

I pushed my ass out, enjoying the feeling of his cock pushing between my legs. He was hard and ready for me, and if I was being honest, I couldn't really think of any reason this didn't qualify as a shower.

"The last time I was in here, you weren't this friendly," I moaned.

"The last time you were in here, you were hiding from me," he answered. "And you were in here without my permission. I wanted to jump into that tub with you and have my way with you. At the time, however, I didn't think it was part of our contract."

I pushed against him, the thrill of need running from my center down my legs the closer he got to taking me. "And now?"

"Now," he growled, "our contract is over, and I'm starting to think that you might want me more than I realized."

The tip of his cocked brushed against my clit, and I gasped, rocking my hips for him.

My attention caught on what he'd said about our contract being over. But that thought fled my mind when he pushed into me and started moving, his hands grasping mine and taking them over my head against the wall while he held me there and fucked me from behind, his teeth on my neck and his breath soft and gasping in my ear.

• • ⚜ • •

I DIDN'T HAVE ONE SINGLE idea how I was going to face his mother and father after what I'd just done with their son, but when we met them for breakfast—a very couple thing to do, I'll note—they were so nice that I didn't have time to be embarrassed.

In fact, they were all questions, and I was so busy coming up with answers that wouldn't give away my identity that I didn't have time for much else.

I talked and laughed and ate, talking and laughing more in between bites, and had the glancing thought that I was mildly jealous of Leo, having grown up with a family who obviously loved him so much. Then I remembered how lonely he said he'd been when he was a kid, and how hard he worked now, just to keep up with what his dad had built, and I realized that it hadn't all been sunshine and rainbows for him, either.

He'd barely seen his parents when he was young, and in that regard, I had the edge on him. My mom and I might have been poor, but we'd also been best friends.

At least before Roger arrived on the scene.

The thought threw an entire pail of cold water on the morning, and I shivered.

Roger. He brought with him a whole host of other thoughts—including the growing need to get away from Leo soon. I'd seen all the press at the auction last night, and I knew for a fact that they'd been taking pictures of Leo and me. It made sense, given the fact that one of the reasons Leo had asked me to help him was that his publicist had told him that he needed to be seen with the same girl more than once for his public image.

I had literally been hired to be that girl on his arm more than once. And for that to have full effect, there needed to be pictures.

But pictures also meant that Roger might see me and recognize me. He might know where I was—and who I was with.

He might come after Leo just to get to me.

All reasons I had to get out of here sooner rather than later. If something happened to Leo because of a man who was chasing after me, I'd never be able to forgive myself.

And I couldn't afford to let myself fall into this happy little domestic thing we had going on between us. I had to stay alert.

I had to get out.

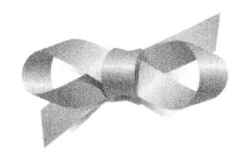

CHAPTER 24

LEO

I WENT BACK TO THE office on Monday feeling like I'd done a whole lot of good things with my weekend—and like I had a whole lot of other good things planned for the coming weeks.

Sure, I didn't know exactly what those good things were yet. But if they included Olivia, I didn't think they could be anything other than wonderful.

Okay, yes, I heard myself, and I knew how that sounded. I knew I'd promised that I wasn't going to get emotionally involved and that I was going to protect myself. I even knew that I'd promised myself—as well as Jack—that I wouldn't do anything else with her until I had the PI's background check safely in hand.

But that was before I'd danced with her at the auction and run my fingers through her hair in bed that night. It was before I'd seen her in that dress and started getting small but still important personal stories from her.

It was before I'd spent the entire weekend either in bed with her or sitting around the house only half-clothed, watching a movie or playing a game.

In short, it was before I'd spent the weekend catching feelings for her despite my promises to keep my emotions in check when it came to the girl who wouldn't tell me anything about who she really was.

Of course, the moment I walked into my office and saw Meghan waiting for me, my head came right out of the cloud it had been inhabiting all weekend. In short, my publicist brought me thumping right back to earth—before she even said anything.

Once she said something, it was even worse.

"Look at this," she said, bringing her forefinger down hard on the papers I could now see spread across my desk in front of her. "There's a big story about the charity auction right here. And it lists the donors. And guess who's not on the list?"

I scoffed at this, because I'd already fixed this problem. "I *did* donate. Ten million, as it happens."

She gave me a serious look and then glanced down at the papers again. "And yet your name isn't on this list. In fact..." She ran her finger through the column, pretending to be speed-reading it. Which was a lie, I knew.

She'd probably already read it so much that she had the damn thing memorized.

"There's no mention of you at all in this particular story," she finished, turning her eyes back up to me.

At that, though, I scoffed again. "That's not possible. There were tons of photographers there, and they were taking pictures like crazy."

"Oh, pictures I have." She jerked the top newspaper off the stack and slid several others toward me.

I glanced down and saw picture after picture—in both black and white and color—of Olivia and me. Us entering the event, her eyes enormous as she realized just what she'd signed up for. Us looking down on the ballroom and me pointing—to the group of people we had to talk to, I supposed. Her smiling up at me as I talked seriously to her—probably promising her a dance and all the champagne she could drink if she behaved herself.

Us dancing, her head resting on my chest and my hand clutching her back possessively. My face, only slightly less possessive, as I looked down on her like she was the most wonderful thing I'd ever seen in my entire life.

"They really did get everything, didn't they?" I asked, smiling at the memory of how she'd felt in my arms.

To my surprise, Meghan scowled. "They did, and it's a good thing, too, because you being there with a girl at least makes the board like you a little bit more. And the press. The press certainly liked her."

She slid another paper forward, and I read the title of the lead story: *Minneapolis Playboy Finds True Love with Gorgeous Mystery Woman.*

"Mystery woman?" I asked, laughing. "Olivia is going to love that."

"Well, she's only a mystery until people figure out that she's also your newest accountant," Meghan muttered. "She is, right? The girl you just hired to head up the accounting department?"

"She is, but that was an afterthought," I said defensively. "I needed someone in that position, and she was the best fit on short notice."

"It still looks like you're dating one of your employees, and that is not a good look," Meghan said sharply. "How exactly do you think you're going to explain that one?"

Dammit.

"I hadn't really thought about it," I admitted. "But surely—"

"Surely nothing," she snapped. "First, you don't donate. Now you look like you're using your company as your own private dating service. The board isn't going to like either of those things, and you know it."

"Well, when you put it that way..."

When she put it that way, I *did* know it. I also hated it.

"And I did donate, by the way," I said. "I just asked that my name not be used."

"So you may as well not have donated at all," she retorted.

I stared at her, shocked. "I would say the kids the money is going to help would have a different opinion. They're getting $10 million worth of supplies. I will never understand why people are so obsessed with knowing who is doing what with their money. It's the outcome that matters, not the prestige."

"According to you, maybe," she said, her voice slightly gentler. "But the board wants the prestige. And for that to happen, you have to start agreeing to people putting your name out there when you've donated."

"Fine," I grumbled. "Anything else?"

She grinned. "I thought you'd never ask." She slid a white card across the desk to me. "We have an art auction coming up. I expect you to take a date. And buy something. Publicly."

I glanced at the invitation. Take a date. Buy something. Publicly. I could do that.

"Any rules about who this date should be?" I asked, pretending innocence.

She scowled at me. "The same girl you took to the charity auction. I don't like that she works here, but we need consistency. We'll worry about the ethics later."

She left before I could answer her, her last line ringing in my ears.

We'll worry about the ethics later.

If people didn't like that I was dating an employee, they'd like it even less if they knew that I'd found her living in her car in an alley.

I was going to have to come up with a better story for how I'd met her if we were going to keep making appearances together.

I was also going to have to come up with a way to convince her to stay longer.

I wondered if she'd do it if I just asked. Or if she needed a reason more than just me.

CHAPTER 25

OLIVIA

• • ⚜ • •

I GLANCED AT THE CLOCK on my computer and grinned to myself. It was almost lunch, and I'd had a really terrific morning in terms of getting shit done. I was actually starting to think I might be good at this whole corporate thing after all. I'd gone through all the processes in the accounting department at this point and had made so many improvements I thought I probably already deserved a raise. I'd even met the CFO—one Jack Reading—and had impressed him so much he'd spent more time just staring at me and shaking his head than actually answering my questions.

Then the grin died, because I remembered that it was lunchtime.

And I'd set myself a very specific goal for this particular lunch.

It had been over a week since I'd spoken with my mother, and I missed her like crazy. Yes, Alice was keeping an eye on her and giving me updates every time we spoke. But it wasn't the same. I wanted to hear her voice. Hear that she was okay and that she was at least close to happy.

I wanted her to hear from me, too, because I'd left town without bothering to give her any heads-up, and I hadn't even left a note. Honestly, I'd been too freaked-out by Roger and what he'd said.

Freaked-out that if he found a note from me to my mother, he would have taken it out on my mother.

I already knew he was looking for me. Alice had said as much. I didn't want to get into it with him, and I certainly didn't want to make it any worse for anyone left at home.

But crap, I missed my mom. I missed her sweet, slightly scattered voice and the way she always forgot whether she'd already told you something or not. I missed her constant nagging about me finding a nice guy and the fact that I was so much better at numbers than she was that I'd taken over balancing her checkbook when I was ten.

I missed my mom. And I wanted to talk to her badly enough that I was willing to take the risk of calling.

But I wasn't going to use the cell phone Leo had bought me, and I sure wasn't going to use the phone at my desk. Far too much chance of either of those showing up with an ID tag on her cell phone.

So pay phone it was. I'd been living on this street for a day before I met Leo and he took me home like a stray, so I knew for a fact that there was a pay phone on the corner. Hell, I even knew the trick for getting the damn door open when it got stuck.

I glanced at the clock again, then took a deep breath, clocked out, and got up. I was nervous as hell about doing this, but waiting around wasn't going to change anything.

If I wanted to talk to my mom, I needed to get a move on.

While praying that no one had the bright idea to follow me out onto the street, where they might notice what I was doing and take it back to Leo himself.

. . ⚜ . .

I SHOULDN'T HAVE BEEN surprised when Roger answered her phone.

Disappointed and furious? Yes. Annoyed as all get out? Absolutely. Worried that something might have happened to her at his hands?

Yep.

But I shouldn't have been surprised.

Luckily, I'd been dodging him for long enough before I even left town that it was second nature now, and I quickly shifted into *Don't let Roger know it's me* mode.

"Hello, sir, may I speak with Vicky?" I asked, trying like hell to make my voice sound deeper than it actually was.

"You could if she was here. Olivia," he snarled. "You have some nerve running out on her the way you did and then just calling up one day like you have a right to it."

My defenses came up immediately. And they brought my anger with them. "And you have some nerve answering her fucking cell phone like it belongs to you, Roger," I snarled right back. "Where is she? Why are you answering her phone?"

"Because I'm the one who bought it for her, bitch!" he hissed. "I'll answer her phone when I want to answer her phone. And as for you, you better get your sweet little ass home before I have to come find you. It's going to be a whole lot worse for you if I have to go out of my way."

Fury tore through me like a freight train at his words. He might talk to my mother like that, but he had zero right to talk to me that way, and if he'd been right there in front of me, I would have—

I yanked myself short right there. I couldn't say what I wanted to because he might take it out on my mom. Scratch that. He definitely would take it out on my mom. There was no question about it.

And he knew I knew that. He'd be counting on that knowledge to have me running home, just to shelter her from whatever he was going to do. He had me in a corner, and he fucking knew it. I didn't know what he wanted with me or why, but he knew he was putting me in an impossible situation.

I couldn't go home again.

I also couldn't leave my mom there by herself.

And I definitely couldn't answer him. I'd never been good at keeping my emotions under control when I spoke. My anger would show too clearly through my voice.

So I did the only thing I *could* do. I slammed the phone down before I let any of the anger bleed out into my words. And then I turned and slammed out of the phone booth.

And ran right into Leo Folley, who evidently hung out around this phone booth so often that if I went into the booth, I was bound to run into him when I came back out again.

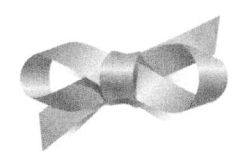

CHAPTER 26

LEO

I LOOKED FROM THE TINY, flushed woman in front of me to the booth she'd just come out of—which I now realized I'd been walking past every time I went to lunch at my favorite diner—and frowned.

"Strange place to hang out on your lunch break, but I guess if you're into it..." I joked.

She flushed even darker, if that were possible, and glanced with a whole lot of guilt back at the phone booth in question. "Um, yeah..."

Right, well, I hadn't been going to ask about it before, but the guilty look on her face immediately put my guard up. This was a woman I already wasn't sure I could trust—though I desperately wanted to—and now I was catching her coming out of a phone booth in the middle of the day and definitely looking like she'd been doing something she shouldn't be doing.

"So this is where I say, 'of all the gin joints in all the world,' or something like that," I told her. "At least that's what I'd say if I was cool enough to even know what that line comes from."

"A movie," she said with a smirk. "*Casablanca*, actually. Though I'm not sure if you're cool enough to remember that."

"Definitely not," I admitted. I'd never been that good at trivia. "The more important question is what you were doing in the same phone booth you were in the first time I got run over by you. Nostalgia?"

A defensive wall came down over her face, cutting the blush off at its base. "Would you believe me if I said I was changing into my super-hero costume?"

"No. Not when I know you have a bathroom available to you upstairs. Nice try, Superman."

She pouted a little bit. "Okay, well, I was making a phone call. As you usually do in phone booths."

"A phone call that required a phone booth rather than the cell phone I bought you?" I asked. I was trying to keep my suspicion at bay. I swear.

I just wasn't having that much success at it.

"Is this some sort of top secret phone call that can't be made via cell phone technology or something?" I continued.

Those defensive walls I'd seen on her face before got even taller. "I had to make a call, and I don't have the cell phone on me. I left it upstairs in my desk and was out here for lunch and realized that I needed to make a call. So, you know..."

Okay, now I knew something was going on. That had been legitimate word salad, and Olivia was not the sort of person who dealt in word salad. She was too straightforward for that. I'd never been around her when she was so flustered that she couldn't think of a way out of a situation, and I'd never known her to be anything more than straightforward. She might have lied to me about half of the things she'd told me—I legitimately didn't know—but even lying seemed to be a smooth, natural feeling for her.

Seeing her flustered was what finally pushed me over the edge from slightly curious into completely suspicious.

Like I said, the woman didn't get flustered easily.

"Why don't you bring your cell phone with you when you go to lunch?" I asked, still trying to make it a joke. "I mean, at least for the games."

She huffed. "I can't stand those things. Mindless tasks that you can engineer your way out of almost immediately."

I actually laughed at that one, though I could see right through the joke. "I don't even know if I can pretend to be surprised by that. Still..."

I grabbed my own phone, hit one of the last numbers I'd dialed, and held it to my ear.

Her phone rang inside her purse.

I tried to keep my face as neutral as possible, though alarm bells were now blaring through my head. "So you actually just don't want to use the cell phone you very clearly have with you."

She... grinned.

And I'm talking a bright, flashy grin. The first non-blushing expression I'd seen from her since she stepped out of the phone booth and right onto my left foot.

And after a solid five minutes of her being so flustered she could hardly speak straight, the grin was... telling. She'd found her footing again. No longer flustered.

Completely comfortable.

"Just trying to keep the mystery alive," she said smoothly. "Wouldn't want you to get bored. I'm actually on my way to lunch, though, so I won't keep you any longer. I'm sure you've got important running of the company to do. I'll talk to you later."

She scooted past me and down the block so quickly that by the time I got over the shock of her words and turned around to look for her, she'd already turned the corner.

Right into the alley where I'd found her.

Which reminded me—forcibly—that this was a girl I'd found living in her car down that alley, without a penny to her name (I had assumed) and definitely without any friends in the city.

I'd thought at the time that she'd been hiding from something—or someone—and that feeling was now growing by leaps and bounds.

Sleeping in her car rather than checking into a hotel. Jumpy about letting anyone near her.

Refusing to use a cell phone, and when I finally forced one on her, refusing to program numbers into it.

Something was definitely going on. And here, the conflict was real, because while one side of my head was telling me that I needed to figure out what that something was, the other side was reminding me how much I liked this girl.

I was genuinely starting to care for her. Depend on her.

I was definitely starting to like having her around. And I'd been making plans—though not solid ones—for how to keep her.

But this episode, and the outright secretiveness, was making one thing very clear: if I was going to keep her, I was going to need to know exactly who she was—and where she'd been, and what she was running from.

。。⚜。。

I STARED DOWN AT THE paperwork Olivia had filled out when she signed the NDA with the company and sighed. I hadn't wanted to do this. The truth was, I'd dragged my feet horribly about it.

To the point that Jack had almost done it without me.

But the deeper I got into this thing, and the more I started to care for her, the more I realized that I needed to know who Olivia actually was.

I swiveled toward my computer and quickly put in the information I had from the employee file. Olivia Cadwell, from Bloomingdale, Minnesota.

It wasn't much to go on. But Bloomingdale was a relatively small town—which made sense, given her accent. She wasn't from the city. She might have gone to New York for college, but that had been a big jump for her.

Originally, she was from a place where everyone knew everyone else.

I was hoping that would make it easier for the private investigator to find out who she'd been before she got to *my* big city and ended up attracting my attention.

I hit Send on the email I'd been drafting before I could rethink it or talk myself out of it and then picked up the phone on my desk and hit an extension for the accounting department.

"This is Olivia," she answered, sounding very professional and very honest.

I wondered if that was her real name or if her name was something more country. Sharon. Courtney. Alison.

She looked like an Olivia to me. But maybe that was because I'd always known her as one.

"Olivia, it's Leo," I said.

"Oh, the CEO," she murmured, her voice dropping a bit. "Am I in trouble, sir? Do you need to see me in your office?"

The tone of voice and her words had my breath catching in my throat, the blood rushing right to my cock. I felt my body go liquid with sudden need, my fingertips twitching at the memory of how soft her skin was.

Down, boy, I told myself firmly.

This wasn't a girl I was going to let myself flirt with. Or think about. Or want.

Not yet.

"You're not in trouble," I said, smiling. "But I'd like to take you out to dinner tonight. What do you think?"

"Can I wear flip-flops and jeans?"

I rapidly recalculated which restaurant we were going to. "Of course."

"Then you're on, boss."

And she hung up.

I hung up as well, already putting a plan together. I needed answers from Olivia, and I needed them soon. But I really, really liked the girl. I wanted her to be...

I wanted her to be the woman I thought she was.

So I was going to give her a chance to answer my questions before the PI got back to me. And I was going to hope like hell that her answers were good ones.

CHAPTER 27

OLIVIA

MAN, WAS I A GOOD NEGOTIATOR. And I hadn't even had to try that hard.

I mean, I'd just asked if I could wear jeans and flip-flops, and it had resulted in Leo bringing me to the cutest little café I'd ever seen.

The place was all done in light pink, mint green, and gold, along with wrought iron and bronze, and I started planning my macaron order the moment we walked through the door. It looked like the kind of place that put rum in your iced tea and plenty of mint in your mojito.

"I think I might be in love," I told him, sliding into a more-comfortable-than-it-looked wrought-iron chair. I shifted a bit, surprised at the amount of padding they'd managed to shove into this place, and gave him a very satisfied grin.

He, on the other hand, was looking shocked and sort of cornered. "Love? What are you talking about?"

I laughed, too amused at his panicked look to do anything else. "Don't worry, big man—I'm not talking about you. I'm talking about the restaurant. Why haven't we come to this place before?"

"Because it's my secret weapon," he whispered. "My best-kept secret. I don't spring it on people until I really need something. It would be a waste to use it on anything less than important."

My blood, which had been sort of singing with excitement at the beauty of the place, suddenly turned to ice.

"So we're here to discuss something important, then," I said, all joking gone from my voice. "Suddenly, I'm not loving this place as much as I thought I did."

His face melted at that, going from joking to stern and then back again as he had some sort of conversation inside his head about whether he really wanted to do whatever it was he'd thought he wanted to do.

When he spoke, it was somewhere in between joking and serious, like he'd come to compromise.

"What makes you think it's bad important?" he asked. "Maybe it's *good* important."

I put up a finger to tell him to hold that thought because the waiter had arrived, and I ordered a mojito—as quick as it could get here—and the bacon and Gouda grilled cheese sandwich, which sounded completely heavenly.

"Can you add tomatoes?" I asked.

"We can do whatever you want to it, miss," the waiter said with a sneaky smile.

Well, this was going to be fun. "In that case, tomatoes for sure and balsamic vinegar if you have it."

He tipped his head in interest, making me think that my little additions might soon be making a debut on their menu, and then nodded. "That sounds even better. I'll make sure it's done."

He took Leo's order—some sort of steak sandwich that I didn't really listen to—and then scuttled out of there, still making notes on his little pad.

"I find myself completely unsurprised that you add things to a sandwich that already sounds heavenly," Leo noted, chuckling.

I just shrugged. "What can I say? I like what I like. And if I see a way to make something better..."

"That's what I'm hearing from the accounting department, too," he said. "You've been improving everything since you've been there."

Pride crept through my body at his words. Yeah, I'd known I was doing a good job. But there was just something about hearing you were doing a good job from a guy who seemed like he might be hard to please, you know?

Especially when you were very admittedly starting to have feelings for said guy. And had already slept with him several times.

Let him do things to you no one had ever done. Let him make you feel things you didn't think you'd ever feel again.

And thoughts like that were going to make the next couple of days really, really hard.

Because I was planning to leave the man. Pronto. I'd known that before, but I was even more set on the action now that I'd talked to Roger and heard that he was actively searching for me.

I grabbed the mojito from the waiter and took a deep gulp.

Just the right amount of rum. Definitely enough mint.

"Glorious," I told the waiter. Then I turned to Leo. "Hey, I'm here to save the day," I told him honestly. "Here to make your life a little easier."

His smile was so brilliant that it looked like he was advertising whitening toothpaste.

Which made me immediately realize that I'd somehow said exactly what he wanted me to say.

Shit.

The last thing I wanted to do was make him think we were on the same wavelength or something like that. It would make it even more shocking to him when I told him I had to leave.

"What?" I asked suspiciously.

He reached out and actually took my freaking hand.

Double shit. What was going on here? Why did I feel like he was about to propose to me or something?

"I'm actually really glad you said that," he told me. "Because I'm hoping... Well, I'm hoping you'll stay on for a bit longer."

"What?" I repeated, having evidently lost the ability to say anything else.

"The thing is, the position you're in at the office is something really, really important. And I just can't find anyone who seems to fit. Believe me, Janice and I have gone through the resumes. A lot. No one works. But I'm starting to think no one else works because I already have the right person."

"And you're thinking that right person is me?" I asked hoarsely.

"I sure am. It's my job to see these sorts of things, you know."

I... didn't know what to say. I didn't know what to *think*. He wanted me to stay and keep working for him? He wanted to keep me at the head of his accounting department?

I'd been expecting something bad when he said we were going to be having an important conversation. I definitely hadn't been expecting him to offer me a job.

One of the most important jobs in his company.

I took another gulp of mojito and motioned for the waiter to bring me another one. If this sort of conversation kept up, I was going to go through mojitos as quickly as he could bring them.

。。⌒∞⌒。。

BY THE TIME WE GOT back to the apartment—and the room I had thought I would be packing up tomorrow—I was torn between going right to it and continuing with my packing process... and making plans to stay.

I was also very, very drunk.

Leo had been lobbying for me to stay through the entire lunch, and "lobbying" was really the only word for it. He'd laid out about five hundred reasons for me to stay, and though I hated to admit it, they'd all been good ones. Safety. Security. A very, very good job where I had a lot of power.

And the more I drank, the more it started to sound like a pretty good idea.

I'd thought I had a plan. I'd thought I knew exactly what I needed to do. But after a full dinner of being courted by a man who definitely knew how to get people to see things his way...

Well, I was definitely questioning everything.

"But why do you really want me to stay?" I asked again, taking the step onto the marble floor of the apartment's foyer. "You could hire someone else. I know you say you can't, but we both know you could. Someone with an actual degree. And experience. Why are you so set on me staying?"

He took my arm and turned me so quickly that I nearly lost my balance, and then caught me just in time to keep us both from going to the floor. I ended up pressed up against him, my hands on his chest, my face tilted up toward his. I could feel his heart beating hard under my palms, and my own moving to match his.

I could feel him growing hard against my stomach. Not that I'd needed the evidence. His eyes were already telling me very clearly that he wanted me.

"I'm set on you staying," he whispered, "because I want to keep you. Isn't that obvious? Haven't you guessed that yet? I don't want to let you go, Olivia. Yes, I want you to keep working at the company. I think you're brilliant, and I don't think I could replace you even if I tried. But more than that... I want to keep you. Don't go. Stay with me for a little while longer."

He started to say something else but cut it off, and though I wondered fleetingly what he'd been about to tell me—or ask—I didn't wonder for very long.

The moment his lips touched mine, in the softest, gentlest, most bone-melting kiss I'd ever experienced, all thoughts went right out of my head.

All thoughts, that is, except for the one very firm idea that I wanted to stay with this man, too. And that was a very big problem.

CHAPTER 28

OLIVIA

I WOKE UP THE NEXT morning with a hangover.

Not that it was a big surprise, I thought, staring blearily at the ceiling. I must have drunk a whole bottle of rum all by myself at the restaurant last night. I was actually surprised I'd managed to sleep in my own bed rather on the floor of the bathroom.

Or in Leo's bed, where I'd wanted—badly—to end up.

Unfortunately, Leo had taken given me that one deep, searching kiss... and then pulled back and told me that he didn't believe in taking a woman who could hardly stand on her own to bed.

Look, I appreciated it. I really did. I was grateful that he was such an upstanding guy and all that. But at the time, I'd wanted so badly to be taken to bed that I'd gone to my room in a huff at the perceived rejection. And then I'd gone to bed feeling very stupid and very lonely.

Only to wake up with a hangover.

All in all, it hadn't been a banner twelve hours. And now I had to wake up and go to the office to work with numbers. No matter how easy numbers were for me, they weren't that pleasurable with a hangover.

Still, I dragged myself out of bed and through the process of a shower and breakfast, and by the time we left for the office, I was feeling a whole lot more human. I was actually starting to feel pretty good.

Until we got to the office and I saw that the place was fucking surrounded by press. And I mean surrounded. There were so many reporters—and accompanying photographers—that I lost count at twenty-five.

"What the hell is going on here?" I asked, leaning over him and staring out the window.

He was frowning at the reporters like he could send them away with just a look. He hadn't been expecting them, either, and I was thinking that when you were Leo Folley, you got used to things like reporters—but you also got used to them following your rules, showing up only when you asked them to.

If they were here when he hadn't been expecting them, it was because they knew something he didn't.

And shit, they had photographers. Lots and lots of cameras. Which was a very, very big problem for a girl like me, who was doing her very best not to be recognizable to the man back in Bloomingdale who wanted very badly to find her.

"Do we have to go out there?" I asked, my voice a little bit weak.

"Well, we have to get into the office," he said reasonably. "So I think the answer is yes. Come on."

He grabbed my hand and pulled me out of the car before I could say that surely there was a back door into the office we could use, and a moment later, I found myself with my feet on the pavement in front of the building and about a thousand cameras flashing on me.

Damn, the pictures.

I did my best to cover my face, turning it down toward the ground and shielding my eyes, but I knew they'd gotten some good pictures of me before I did that. Not that it mattered, really; they'd taken pictures of me at the charity auction, too, and I'd barely thought about it at the time.

Mostly because I'd been in Leo's arms and thinking about how he made me feel, rather than the things I should be doing to make sure he stayed safe.

Now, though, with my departure right there on the horizon and my mind already made up, this felt completely unfair. I was almost out of here! Why did they have to take pictures of me now? What the hell did they want, anyhow? What was suddenly so interesting about us?

"Leo, are you two sleeping together?" someone suddenly shouted. "Don't you think it's a conflict of interest to be sleeping with one of your employees?"

"Leo!" another voice said. "Isn't this the girl you took to the auction? Were you dating her before you hired her?"

"Leo! What does the board think of you playing with your employees?"

"Is she cooking the books for you?"

And on and on, all in the same vein.

My goodness. I realized they were taking pictures of us because they thought we were dating. And they thought I was working for his company. Which meant he was dating one of his employees—and an employee who handled his books for him.

Yeah, that had "conflict of interest" written all over it. No wonder they were all over him for it.

All over me.

I ducked down more and rushed for the front of the office, praying no one had gotten a good look at my face... and that Roger wouldn't be paying attention to press from Minneapolis or the billionaire who had decided to start dating the accountant he'd just found sleeping in her car in the alley next to his building.

• • ⚜ • •

THE REST OF THE DAY went pretty much the same. Though the people in the office itself were used to the fact that Leo and I were...

well, not just an accountant and her boss, but potentially something more... they were evidently not used to the press becoming a mob in front of the building.

And since I was the reason for it, I became the local celebrity.

It was pure hell for someone who preferred to stay out of the limelight. I'd always managed to keep to myself, and I liked it that way. Having the reporters after me and the people I was working with going outside to talk to those reporters about me and what I might be doing on my time off was exhausting.

It got even worse when Leo emailed me to tell me that he was going into a meeting with the board and would be out of the office for the next hour or so.

My stomach immediately dropped right out of my body and through the floor below me. What was going on? I racked my brain for information but couldn't find any memory of him having said he had a meeting with the board today. Was this something that was happening purely because of all the media coverage?

This was exactly why I hadn't wanted to get involved with his company. Sure, I'd volunteered for it in the first place, but only because I'd thought I could save him, and I certainly hadn't meant to *stay* here. At some point, they were going to find out that we were doing even more than dating, and then they were going to find out how he'd found me and what I'd agreed to, and then they'd find out who I was—I'd heard reporters were good at that sort of thing—and it was all going to be in the papers.

And then Roger would know exactly where to find me.

And he'd know that Leo was the one who'd been protecting me. And he'd go after Leo, too.

Look, I knew with my rational mind that Leo would be just fine. He was a whole lot richer and smarter than Roger was, and it was pretty stupid for me to be worrying about him. First of all, he wasn't mine to protect. Secondly, he could definitely afford to be protected.

He would be fine.

That didn't stop me from feeling horribly guilty for even possibly bringing someone like Roger into his life.

The whole thing led to one very simple conclusion: I had to go. No matter how much I wanted to stay with Leo, or how convincing he'd been when he asked me to stay, I had to go.

He was asking too many questions, and I was catching too many feelings for him, and the situation I'd left back at home was going to explode at some point. Especially if Leo kept poking at it.

I started packing up my desk right then, knowing that I couldn't delay this any longer. I had to get whatever payment Leo was willing to give me, collect my car from the garage where I'd had it parked this entire time, and disappear again.

I didn't think about how I'd be leaving my heart behind me with Leo. I didn't think about how he might be able to protect me from Roger. And I didn't think about how it would feel to be able to stay in that safe, comfortable apartment with a man who made me feel the way he did.

It was better for both of us if I left. And that was all that mattered.

CHAPTER 29

LEO

"SO THE BOARD WANTED to meet with you." Jack's voice didn't hold any emotion or any judgment. It was flat and rational. Just stating the facts.

Just telling me what I already knew.

"They did. They don't like that I'm dating someone who's working here. Or that I hired her without bothering to interview her or inform them. You'd think they owned the company or something."

"Well, they sort of do," he observed, still in that flat voice. "I mean, half of it."

I ground my teeth. "But I own the other half, and at the end of the day, I could buy them out if I wanted to. They don't have any right to tell me how to run the place."

"Only they do, Leo, and you know it." He paused, feeling out how he was going to say whatever it was he had to say, and then jumped in. "I don't know what you're doing with the girl, Leo, and I don't really care. She makes you happy. Any fool could see that. Damn, the look on your face when you were dancing with her at the charity auction... It should have been rated R, is all I'm saying. But she can't be working here. You're going to have to find a replacement for her. Unless you actually find out who she is and where she's been. If you can give them her background—her education, at the very least—I think you can save this. But just having a name that you think is right and her promise that she's aboveboard?" He gave me a hopeless look.

The problem was, I knew he was right. I knew there was a whole lot wrong with the entire situation, and I knew I had to figure out what it was. I'd thought from the very beginning that she was hiding from something.

I needed to know what it was. Before it impacted my company any further.

I'd been supposed to ask her last night at dinner. Give her a chance to clear her own name. But what with one thing and another, and all the drinks, and then that searing kiss...

Well, it had slipped my mind, that was all.

Still, we were going to be alone tonight. I was going to cook her dinner to avoid having to go out with the press. I'd have her to myself, and I couldn't say how much longer that would be true. Tonight, I'd get her to tell me who she was, if only so I could keep her at the company.

I'd just tell her I had to know. Yes, she was annoyed with me for asking questions about her past, and yes, she'd told me that she didn't want to talk about it. Yes, she'd think I was being beyond nosy.

But if she wanted to stay—if she wanted to stay even half as badly as I wanted her to stay—she was going to have to come clean. That was all there was to it.

• • ⚓ • •

I STIRRED ONE POT, then quickly moved to the next and stirred that one. Then I moved to the frying pan and quickly flipped the contents there, turned down the heat, and flipped them again.

I loved cooking, I really did, but when my mind was 75 percent on the woman currently sitting in the living room drinking wine like her life actually depended on it and barely speaking to me, I was cooking at my own risk. And the risk of my apartment. I couldn't seem to keep my attention on the food I was supposed to be supervising.

I also hadn't come up with a plan for how I was going to handle this yet.

"Just ask her to come clean, man," I told myself firmly. "You're not asking for the world. You're just asking for the full story of who she is and what she's doing here. Maybe even how she came to be staying in her car in an alleyway in Minneapolis, rather than doing the normal human thing and looking for a hotel."

"Are you really in here talking to yourself?" a voice asked me from the doorway into the living room.

I jumped, flipping a spoonful of bell peppers into the air, and turned just as those bell pepper slices started hitting the floor.

Olivia watched the entire operation, her mouth twitching and her eyebrows rising up in surprise, and then she started laughing.

I started laughing as well because it was just so ridiculous. I'd just reacted to her coming into the kitchen like I'd been expecting to be shot in the back or something, and in doing so, had managed to spill a good portion of our dinner on the floor.

I immediately grabbed the roll of paper towels and started cleaning up the mess. "I guess we're having less bell pepper in the food than I had originally intended," I muttered.

She dropped to her knees next to me and started helping. "That's okay. I don't actually like bell peppers much to start with."

I glanced up. "Really? Why didn't you say anything when we were at the store? Buying bell peppers?"

She glanced up as well, smiling shyly. "Because I could tell you were excited about whatever you were cooking, and I didn't want to ruin it."

She looked... different when she was shy. Sad, somehow. Like she was thinking something she wasn't saying.

I wondered what it was she was thinking about. I wonder if it had anything to do with her past and whatever had been wrong with her. Or that mysterious phone call she'd been making at the pay phone.

The reason she wouldn't use her cell phone. Or tell me where she'd come from. Or who she belonged to.

This girl had been dodging my questions since the moment I met her, and suddenly I wanted to know everything about her. I wanted to know what her childhood had been like and where she'd gone to school and what she'd majored in and whether she'd liked it. I wanted to meet her parents and her best friend. See the house where she'd grown up.

I wanted to tell her all the same things about myself. I wanted to have a real relationship, rather than this halfway thing we'd had up to this point.

I wanted to actually *know* her.

And that was exactly what I needed to tell her, I realized. It was what I should have told her right from the start.

I reached out and took her hand, threading my fingers through hers and pulling her toward me as I rocked back on my heels and ended up sitting on the floor of the kitchen. I maneuvered her into my lap, her legs straddling mine and her face only inches from me.

"Tell me who you are, Olivia. Tell me where you came from. Please. I want to know you for real. I want this to be real. Please stop hiding from me."

It was stupid and cheesy and really, really badly written. But it was coming straight from my heart. And I watched her face get defensive against my questions... and then sort of melt in acceptance. I watched her decide that she *was* going to tell me, and I felt a thrill of victory—of excitement—run through me.

This was going to work. We were going to make it work.

And then my damned cell phone rang, buzzing so loudly in my pocket that it made me jump—with her in my lap.

"Oh shit, I'm sorry," I muttered, scrambling to turn the thing off.

The damage was done, though, and the moment completely ruined. Olivia was scrambling, too, to get off my lap and up off the floor, her hands brushing her legs off and her face shuttering again as she brought her walls back up around her.

"It's okay, don't worry about it," she said. "I mean, we were only sitting on the floor rather than cleaning up the mess you made. It's probably better that someone interrupted us before we did anything totally insane."

I watched her drawing back into herself, my heart slowly breaking apart at the sight of it, and cursed whoever had called me right then. If it was Jack, calling to check on whether I'd found out who she was yet, I would kill him later. And I'd made sure to do it slowly.

When I yanked out my phone, though, I saw that it wasn't Jack.

It was the PI.

"I've got to take this, I'm afraid," I said, getting to my feet.

Olivia waved me away. "No problem. I'll finish up in here."

I left the kitchen without answering, my phone already at my ear. "Pete," I breathed. "Do you have something for me?"

If he could tell me who she was, give me enough to satisfy the board, I could save this. I could make the case for keeping her on and convince her to stay.

I could give her time to tell me her story, rather than forcing it right now.

"Not really," the voice on the other end of the line said flatly. "Though you're still going to have to pay me."

I frowned. "Not really? What does that mean?"

"It means that I didn't find one damn thing. I searched everyone in Bloomingdale. I searched anyone who's lived there for the last fifty years. There's no Olivia Cadwell, twenty-six years old or otherwise. No Cadwells live in that town, and it's small enough that the search only took me half an hour. It went so fast that I searched three times, just to be sure. Even expanded the parameters to search the county around it, just in case she was actually a country girl. That girl didn't come from that town, Leo. I don't know who she is or where she came from, but it looks to me like she's lying on all accounts."

"What?" I breathed, my world shattering to pieces around me.

"She doesn't exist," he said. "At least, not in the persona of Olivia Cadwell."

I hung up the phone, so dazed that I didn't know what to think. When I looked up again, I saw Olivia standing in front of me, and it didn't take much to guess, based on her expression, that she knew exactly what I'd just heard. Maybe she'd been able to hear his voice, or maybe she'd just been expecting that I'd have her searched.

Whatever it was, she knew I'd just found out that she wasn't who she'd been saying she was.

"Leo," she said simply, her voice shaking and her face pale. "I can explain."

THE END

The Millionaire's Pretty Woman Series

Book 1 – Perfect Stranger
Book 2 – Captive Devotion
Book 3 – Sweet Temptations

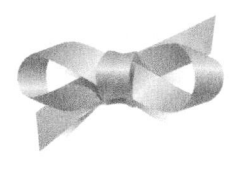

Strength & Style Series

NOW AVAILABLE!!
Book 1 – Suits You, Sir
Book 2 – Tailor Made
Book 3 – Perfect Gentleman

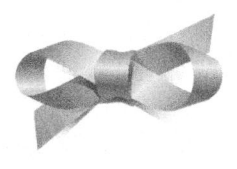

Find Lexy Timms:

LEXY TIMMS NEWSLETTER:
http://eepurl.com/9i0vD
Lexy Timms Facebook Page:
https://www.facebook.com/SavingForever
Lexy Timms Website:
http://www.lexytimms.com

Want

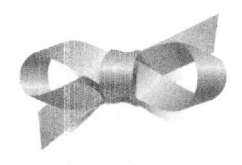

FREE READS?

Sign up for Lexy Timms' newsletter
And she'll send you updates on new releases,
ARC copies of books and a whole lotta fun!

Sign up for news and updates!
http://eepurl.com/9i0vD

More by Lexy Timms:

FROM BEST SELLING AUTHOR, Lexy Timms, comes a billionaire romance that'll make you swoon and fall in love all over again.

Jamie Connors has given up on men. Despite being smart, pretty, and just slightly overweight, she's a magnet for the kind of guys that don't stay around.

Her sister's wedding is at the foreground of the family's attention. Jamie would be fine with it if her sister wasn't pressuring her to lose weight so she'll fit in the maid of honor dress, her mother would get off her case and her ex-boyfriend wasn't about to become her brother-in-law.

Determined to step out on her own, she accepts a PA position from billionaire Alex Reid. The job includes an apartment on his property and gets her out of living in her parent's basement.

Jamie must balance her life and somehow figure out how to manage her billionaire boss, without falling in love with him.

** The Boss is book 1 in the Managing the Bosses series. All your questions won't be answered in the first book. It may end on a cliff hanger.

For mature audiences only. There are adult situations, but this is a love story, NOT erotica.

Book 1 – Payment for Sin
Book 2 – Atonement Within
Book 3 – Declaration of Love

Faking It Description:

HE GROANED. THIS WAS torture. Being trapped in a room with a beautiful woman was just about every man's fantasy, but he had to remember that this was just pretend.

Allyson Smith has crushed on her boss for years, but never dared to make a move. When she finds herself without a date to her brother's upcoming wedding, Allyson tells her family one innocent white lie: that she's been dating her boss. Unfortunately, her boss discovers her lie, and insists on posing as her boyfriend to escort her to the wedding.

Playboy billionaire Dane Prescott always has a new heiress on his arm, but he can't get his assistant Allyson out of his head. He's fought his attraction to her, until he gets caught up in her scheme of a fake relationship.

One passionate weekend with the boss has Allyson Smith questioning everything she believes in. Falling for a wealthy playboy like Dane is against the rules, but if she's just faking it what's the harm?

SOMETIMES THE HEART needs a different kind of saving... find out if Charity Thompson will find a way of saving forever in this hospital setting Best-Selling Romance by Lexy Timms

PERFECT STRANGER

Charity Thompson wants to save the world, one hospital at a time. Instead of finishing med school to become a doctor, she chooses a different path and raises money for hospitals – new wings, equipment, whatever they need. Except there is one hospital she would be happy to never set foot in again—her fathers. So of course, he hires her to create a gala for his sixty-fifth birthday. Charity can't say no. Now she is working in the one place she doesn't want to be. Except she's attracted to Dr. Elijah Bennet, the handsome playboy chief.

Will she ever prove to her father that's she's more than a med school dropout? Or will her attraction to Elijah keep her from repairing the one thing she desperately wants to fix?

THE ONE YOU CAN'T FORGET

Emily Rose Dougherty is a good Catholic girl from mythical Walkerville, CT. She had somehow managed to get herself into a heap trouble with the law, all because an ex-boyfriend has decided to make things difficult.

Luke "Spade" Wade owns a Motorcycle repair shop and is the Road Captain for Hades' Spawn MC. He's shocked when he reads in the paper that his old high school flame has been arrested. She's always been the one he couldn't forget.

Will destiny let them find each other again? Or what happens in the past, best left for the history books?

*** This is book 1 of the Hades' Spawn MC Series. All your questions may not be answered in the first book.*

BILLIONAIRE BIKER
LEXY TIMMS
Download For
FREE
Lexy
Timms

• • ❧ • •

THE
DEAD OF NIGHT
SERIES
LEXY TIMMS
Abduction
Bribery
Corruption

THE
HEAT OF NIGHT
SERIES
USA TODAY BESTSELLING AUTHOR
LEXY TIMMS
Depravity
Scandal
Disgrace

Don't miss out!

Visit the website below and you can sign up to receive emails whenever Lexy Timms publishes a new book. There's no charge and no obligation.

https://books2read.com/r/B-A-NNL-UBAQB

BOOKS 2 READ

Connecting independent readers to independent writers.

Did you love *Perfect Stranger*? Then you should read *Suits You, Sir*[1] by Lexy Timms!

Every great design begins with an even better story...

When I designed my first suit, I never imagined it would lead to the kind of success I've found. The popularity of my company is soaring, the orders rolling in, and there's no sign of slowing down. It's amazing!

But, when my assistant decides to leave, I need to replace her fast. As soon Noelle walks through the door, I know she is exactly what I want, in more ways than one. Her organization, brilliant eye, and refreshingly blunt style has me falling hard and I go so far as to change company bylaws to ensure I can pursue her. But with success comes unwanted attention.

---

1. https://books2read.com/u/4Nwz9x

2. https://books2read.com/u/4Nwz9x

I've tried to keep my company and personal life out of the media, but it isn't easy with a vindictive ex trying to convince everyone she is actually the brains behind my company. I have more to defend now and I'll do anything I have to do it.

Strength & Style Series

Book 1 – Suits You, Sir

Book 2 – Tailor Made

Book 3 – Perfect Gentleman

Read more at www.lexytimms.com.

Also by Lexy Timms

A Bad Boy Bullied Romance
I Hate You
I Hate You A Little Bit
I Hate You A Little Bit More

A Bump in the Road Series
Expecting Love
Selfless Act
Doctor's Orders

A Burning Love Series
Spark of Passion
Flame of Desire
Blaze of Ecstasy

A Chance at Forever Series
Forever Perfect
Forever Desired

Forever Together

A Dark Mafia Romance Series
Taken By The Mob Boss
Truce With The Mob Boss
Taking Over the Mob Boss
Trouble For The Mob Boss
Tailored By The Mob Boss
Tricking the Mob Boss

A Dating App Series
I've Been Matched
You've Been Matched
We've Been Matched

A "Kind of" Billionaire
Taking a Risk
Safety in Numbers
Pretend You're Mine

A Maybe Series
Maybe I Should
Maybe I Shouldn't
Maybe I Did

Assisting the Boss Series
Billion Reasons
Duke of Delegation
Late Night Meetings
Delegating Love
Suitors and Admirers

BBW Romance Series
Capturing Her Beauty
Pursuing Her Dreams
Tracing Her Curves

Beating the Biker Series
Making Her His
Making the Break
Making of Them

Betrayal at the Bay Series
Devil's Bay
Devil's Deceit
Devil's Duplicity

Billionaire Banker Series
Banking on Him

Price of Passion
Investing in Love
Knowing Your Worth
Treasured Forever
Banking on Christmas
Billionaire Banker Box Set Books #1-3

Billionaire CEO Brothers
Tempting the Player
Late Night Boardroom
Reviewing the Perfomance
Result of Passion
Directing the Next Move
Touching the Assets

Billionaire Hitman Series
The Hit
The Job
The Run

Billionaire Holiday Romance Series
Driving Home for Christmas
The Valentine Getaway
Cruising Love
Billionaire Holiday Romance Box Set

Billionaire in Disguise Series
Facade
Illusion
Charade

Billionaire Secrets Series
The Secret
Freedom
Courage
Trust
Impulse
Billionaire Secrets Box Set Books #1-3

Blind Sight Series
See Me
Fix Me
Eyes On Me

Branded Series
Money or Nothing
What People Say
Give and Take

Building Billions

Building Billions - Part 1
Building Billions - Part 2
Building Billions - Part 3

Butler & Heiress Series
To Serve
For Duty
No Chore
All Wrapped Up

Change of Heart Series
The Heart Needs
The Heart Wants
The Heart Knows

Counting the Billions
Counting the Days
Counting On You
Counting the Kisses

Cry Wolf Reverse Harem Series
Beautiful & Wild
Misunderstood
Never Tamed

Darkest Night Series
Savage
Vicious
Brutal
Sinful
Fierce

Diamond in the Rough Anthology
Billionaire Rock
Billionaire Rock - part 2

Dirty Little Taboo Series
Flirting Touch
Denying Pleasure
Forbidding Desire
Craving Passion

Dominating PA Series
Her Personal Assistant - Part 1
Her Personal Assistant - Part 2
Her Personal Assistant Box Set

Fake Billionaire Series
Faking It

Temporary CEO
Caught in the Act
Never Tell A Lie
Fake Christmas
Fake Billionaire Box Set #1-3

Firehouse Romance Series
Caught in Flames
Burning With Desire
Craving the Heat
Firehouse Romance Complete Collection

Forging Billions Series
Dirty Money
Petty Cash
Payment Required

For His Pleasure
Elizabeth
Georgia
Madison

Fortune Riders MC Series
Billionaire Biker
Billionaire Ransom
Billionaire Misery

Fortune Riders Box Set - Books #1-3

Fragile Series
Fragile Touch
Fragile Kiss
Fragile Love

Great Temptation Series
The Devil's Footsteps
Heaven's Command
Mortals Surrender

Hades' Spawn Motorcycle Club
One You Can't Forget
One That Got Away
One That Came Back
One You Never Leave
One Christmas Night
Hades' Spawn MC Complete Series

Hard Rocked Series
Rhyme
Harmony
Lyrics

Heart of Stone Series
The Protector
The Guardian
The Warrior

Heart of the Battle Series
Celtic Viking
Celtic Rune
Celtic Mann
Heart of the Battle Series Box Set

Heistdom Series
Master Thief
Goldmine
Diamond Heist
Smile For Me
Your Move
Green With Envy
Saving Money

Highlander Wolf Series
Pack Run
Pack Land
Pack Rules

Hollyweird Fae Series
Inception of Gold
Disruption of Magic
Guardians of Twilight

How To Love A Spy
The Secret
The Secret Life
The Secret Wife

Just About Series
About Love
About Truth
About Forever
Just About Box Set Books #1-3

Justice Series
Seeking Justice
Finding Justice
Chasing Justice
Pursuing Justice
Justice - Complete Series

Karma Series

Walk Away
Make Him Pay
Perfect Revenge

Kissed by Billions
Kissed by Passion
Kissed by Desire
Kissed by Love

Leaning Towards Trouble
Trouble
Discord
Tenacity

Love on the Sea Series
Ships Ahoy
Rough Sea
High Tide

Love You Series
Love Life
Need Love
My Love

Managing the Billionaire

Never Enough
Worth the Cost
Secret Admirers
Chasing Affection
Pressing Romance
Timeless Memories
Managing the Billionaire Box Set Books #1-3

Managing the Bosses Series
The Boss
The Boss Too
Who's the Boss Now
Love the Boss
I Do the Boss
Wife to the Boss
Employed by the Boss
Brother to the Boss
Senior Advisor to the Boss
Forever the Boss
Christmas With the Boss
Billionaire in Control
Billionaire Makes Millions
Billionaire at Work
Precious Little Thing
Priceless Love
Valentine Love
The Cost of Freedom
Trick or Treat
The Night Before Christmas
Gift for the Boss - Novella 3.5
Managing the Bosses Box Set #1-3

Managing the Bosses Novellas

Mislead by the Bad Boy Series
Deceived
Provoked
Betrayed

Model Mayhem Series
Shameless
Modesty
Imperfection

Moment in Time
Highlander's Bride
Victorian Bride
Modern Day Bride
A Royal Bride
Forever the Bride

Mountain Millionaire Series
Close to the Ridge
Crossing the Bluff
Climbing the Mount

My Best Friend's Sister

Hometown Calling
A Perfect Moment
Thrown in Together

My Darker Side Series
Darkest Hour
Time to Stop
Against the Light

Neverending Dream Series
Neverending Dream - Part 1
Neverending Dream - Part 2
Neverending Dream - Part 3
Neverending Dream - Part 4
Neverending Dream - Part 5
Neverending Dream Box Set Books #1-3

Outside the Octagon
Submit
Fight
Knockout

Protecting Diana Series
Her Bodyguard
Her Defender
Her Champion

Her Protector
Her Forever
Protecting Diana Box Set Books #1-3

Protecting Layla Series
His Mission
His Objective
His Devotion

Racing Hearts Series
Rush
Pace
Fast

Regency Romance Series
The Duchess Scandal - Part 1
The Duchess Scandal - Part 2

Reverse Harem Series
Primals
Archaic
Unitary

R&S Rich and Single Series
Alex Reid

Parker
Sebastian

Saving Forever
Saving Forever - Part 1
Saving Forever - Part 2
Saving Forever - Part 3
Saving Forever - Part 4
Saving Forever - Part 5
Saving Forever - Part 6
Saving Forever Part 7
Saving Forever - Part 8
Saving Forever Boxset Books #1-3

Secrets & Lies Series
Strange Secrets
Evading Secrets
Inspiring Secrets
Lies and Secrets
Mastering Secrets
Alluring Secrets
Secrets & Lies Box Set Books #1-3

Shifting Desires Series
Jungle Heat
Jungle Fever
Jungle Blaze

Sin Series
Payment for Sin
Atonement Within
Declaration of Love

Southern Romance Series
Little Love Affair
Siege of the Heart
Freedom Forever
Soldier's Fortune

Spanked Series
Passion
Playmate
Pleasure

Spelling Love Series
The Author
The Book Boyfriend
The Words of Love

Strength & Style
Suits You, Sir
Tailor Made

Taboo Wedding Series
He Loves Me Not
With This Ring
Happily Ever After

Tattooist Series
Confession of a Tattooist
Surrender of a Tattooist
Heart of a Tattooist
Hopes & Dreams of a Tattooist

Tennessee Romance
Whisky Lullaby
Whisky Melody
Whisky Harmony

The Bad Boy Alpha Club
Battle Lines - Part 1
Battle Lines

The Brush Of Love Series
Every Night
Every Day
Every Time

Every Way
Every Touch
The Brush of Love Series Box Set Books #1-3

The City of Mayhem Series
True Mayhem
Relentless Chaos

The Debt
The Debt: Part 1 - Damn Horse
The Debt: Complete Collection

The Fire Inside Series
Dare Me
Defy Me
Burn Me

The Gentleman's Club Series
Gambler
Player
Wager

The Golden Mail
Hot Off the Press
Extra! Extra!

Read All About It
Stop the Press
Breaking News
This Just In
The Golden Mail Box Set Books #1-3

The Lucky Billionaire Series
Lucky Break
Streak of Luck
Lucky in Love

The Millionaire's Pretty Woman Series
Perfect Stranger
Captive Devotion
Sweet Temptations

The Sound of Breaking Hearts Series
Disruption
Destroy
Devoted

The University of Gatica Series
The Recruiting Trip
Faster
Higher
Stronger

Dominate
No Rush
University of Gatica - The Complete Series

T.N.T. Series
Troubled Nate Thomas - Part 1
Troubled Nate Thomas - Part 2
Troubled Nate Thomas - Part 3

Toxic Touch Series
Noxious
Lethal
Willful
Tainted
Craved
Toxic Touch Box Set Books #1-3

Undercover Boss Series
Marketing
Finance
Legal

Undercover Series
Perfect For Me
Perfect For You
Perfect For Us

Unknown Identity Series
Unknown
Unpublished
Unexposed
Unsure
Unwritten
Unknown Identity Box Set: Books #1-3

Unlucky Series
Unlucky in Love
UnWanted
UnLoved Forever

War Torn Letters Series
My Sweetheart
My Darling
My Beloved

Wet & Wild Series
Stormy Love
Savage Love
Secure Love

Worth It Series

Worth Billions
Worth Every Cent
Worth More Than Money

You & Me - A Bad Boy Romance
Just Me
Touch Me
Kiss Me

Standalone
Wash
Loving Charity
Summer Lovin'
Love & College
Billionaire Heart
First Love
Frisky and Fun Romance Box Collection
Beating Hades' Bikers
Everyone Loves a Bad Boy

Watch for more at www.lexytimms.com.

About the Author

"Love should be something that lasts forever, not is lost forever." Visit USA TODAY BESTSELLING AUTHOR, LEXY TIMMS https://www.facebook.com/SavingForever *Please feel free to connect with me and share your comments. I love connecting with my readers.* Sign up for news and updates and freebies - I like spoiling my readers! http://eepurl.com/9i0vD website: www.lexytimms.com Dealing in Antique Jewelry and hanging out with her awesome hubby and three kids, Lexy Timms loves writing in her free time. MANAGING THE BOSSES is a bestselling 10-part series dipping into the lives of Alex Reid and Jamie Connors. Can a secretary really fall for her billionaire boss?

Read more at www.lexytimms.com.

Printed in Great Britain
by Amazon